NONE SO BLIND

NONE SO BLIND

J. Á. GONZÁLEZ SAINZ

*Translated from the Spanish by
Harold Augenbraum and Cecilia Ross*

Hispabooks Publishing, S. L.
Madrid, Spain
www.hispabooks.com

Originally published in Spain as *Ojos que no ven* by Anagrama, 2010
First published in English by Hispabooks, 2015
English translation copyright © by Harold Augenbraum and Cecilia Ross
Design © simonpates - www.patesy.com

ISBN 978-84-943496-5-2 (trade paperback)
ISBN 978-84-943496-6-9 (ebook)
Legal Deposit: M-6008-2015

For José Ramón González García,
Augustín García Simón, and Ramón Aguirre Urruchúa

We have slipped our backbone; we have about decided a man don't need a backbone any more; to have one is old-fashioned. But the groove where the backbone used to be is still there, and the backbone has been kept alive, too, and someday we're going to slip back onto it. I don't know just when nor just how much of a wrench it will take to teach us, but someday.

WILLIAM FAULKNER

PART ONE

1

It was the first day he'd gone back to doing what some people said he should probably never have stopped doing in the first place, the first day he'd gone back, drawn by the force of something that had held him in thrall for so long, to jumping out of bed in the still-small darkness and making himself, all on his own now, a large, black coffee, and his thick slices of bread and honey, and the first day he'd gone back, in the nascent light of dawn, like so many times before, long ago, when the brightness seemed to light up once more the same things that dusk had left confused and spent and so very, very tired and gave the impression that it would go on lighting them forever, to throwing his worn jacket and his old satchel from twenty years ago over his shoulder and heading off toward the river's silence and his work in the field.

He was relieved when he realized that the road was the same as it had always been. They hadn't redone anything yet or built anything in the area, and when he walked along that road, walking as if it were in fact the road that were walking through him, he was infused with a strange sense of calm and a strange feeling of liberation. It must be that what's permanent, he said to himself, that what will always be the same no matter how many things change, as his father used to say, or as people said his father used to say, is what actually frees you the most. Things that remain the same speak to you, sustain you, and they do it without ego. Although knowing how to listen to them is something else entirely.

But when he got to the field, it had all gone to seed, it was abandoned, godforsaken, he said to himself. Blackberry bushes blocked the path that went down to the work shed and made getting in difficult. The property markers had strayed out of place, and the river seemed to have eaten into part of the property. Clumps of weeds had taken up residence everywhere and seemed to have arranged themselves in strict accordance with the severe dryness of the earth, paradoxically, since they were at the very bank of the river.

Forsaken by God, godforsaken, he repeated several times to himself, perhaps thinking about something more than this piece of land as he gripped the sickle and dug the hoe in to clear the path and get to the doorway, to resituate the property markers, and to begin little by little to bring order to the land. But why would you say godforsaken, when it is we who have forsaken it and let it go to seed, we who cultivate it and improve it and make things grow, and we also who impoverish it and destroy it and let it go to seed, he asked himself. Perhaps it is His hand that puts the hoe in ours to resituate the property markers or make the soil produce, so perhaps it's also His hand that sometimes gives us a hoe, but other times it's not a hoe or a shovel or a rake but, on the contrary—and only He knows why—it's a gun. And if one hand puts something in another hand, if God's hand puts something in our hands, do God's eyes put hate and rancor and ridiculous stubbornness in our eyes, as well?

As the afternoon unfolded, the same way it had twenty years ago, the same way, curiously, that it had the very day he ended his almost daily journeys along that road he had walked for what might accurately be termed as long as he could remember, the weather had suddenly gotten stormy. The sky had been impeccably blue, clear as you could ever imagine, but had given way, just as on that other day, to a cottony landscape of ever more threatening clouds. So he hurried and finished gathering everything up, turned the key in the shed's old, wooden door, which time and lack of care had turned completely gray, and without missing a beat, exhausted as he was, he turned from the shed and went up the path, which was now newly unobstructed and flanked by patches of elder, bisnaga, and danewort, to the road that would take him back to the village.

When he was on the verge of reaching the streets on the outskirts of the village, a bit more or less like on that other day twenty years ago, which was a very different day and yet such a mirror image of this one, a hurricane-force wind began to blow, and all of sudden it swept everything up and sent everything haywire. As if it could no longer bear to have things where they were, the wind began to kick up little whirlwinds of dust and dirt everywhere and every which way; tumbleweeds and gritty particulates, like multiple BB blasts, stuck like tiny needles in his cheeks and forehead, and the dust, the dust everywhere, as if everything had been turned into dust, it got into the corners of his eyes as if to ensure that nothing at all could remain safeguarded from that vortex.

From the outset, pieces of paper and plastic bags began flying through the air along with the grass and the dry leaves the wind was worrying from place to place. You could hear doors slamming inside houses, things falling and banging, glass breaking, and an empty soda can rattling and bouncing and rolling around back and forth, as only emptiness can rattle and roll, seemed to add a metallic hollowness to all the chaos. It would have been difficult to imagine, as it always is, even in the final moments before something throws everything into a frenzy, all the things that could possibly totter, could fall and break, or simply disappear, or shut down in an instant—all the things that could possibly go wrong. Only the plastic bags, inflated and puffy, had a hard time coming back to earth; they were full of the very thing that was sending everything else out of control, and so, molding themselves as fully as possible to that which was scattering everything else, they remained airborne for a long time, buffeted by the whims of the windstorm. They looked like certain people, or certain things, he thought then, as he watched the bags fill up with air and the empty can rattle around, with a sad smile that his tiredness made even sadder.

Then suddenly—there was no one left out on the street—an abrupt fall in the temperature preceded the first isolated drops, giant, fat drops, of a girth so incomprehensibly fat that they pounded into the dust that had piled up on the roads over the course of weeks and weeks of drought with a muted sound, muffled and dull, as if they were smothering something spread out and thin. The worst thing might not be so much what's happening now, no matter how dreadful that may be— Felipe Díaz Carrión said to himself, thinking not just about end-of-summer storms—but the fact that the particulates and dust are shaken free and get into your eyes and blind you, and then anything can happen, anything.

2

What does this coincidence mean, he had wondered during the entire walk back to his house, and even before then, from the very moment that day when he had begun to sense, just as he had twenty years ago, the storm that was now raging around him; do things mean anything, or do they merely happen and we're the ones who implore them to say something to us?

You could get from his house on the outskirts of the village to the shed in the field near the river in two different ways. Along the road on the opposite side of the river, which led to a ford where, on normal days, summer days especially, you could wade through the water with no problem, or along the old bridle trail that ran parallel to the river on the same side as his field. His grandfather, as he remembered vividly, and his father, whose name he always followed with *may he rest in peace* when he mentioned him, and later he himself when he was a child and then a young adult, right up until that equally stormy day twenty years ago when he turned the key in the old, wooden door to return afterward only from time to time in the summer, had all invariably taken the dirt road that went parallel to the river, every time.

Having emerged from the outskirts of the village where they lived, you would immediately cross the old stone bridge, and while still on the little asphalt roadway, you would come to the old abandoned mill. At that point the asphalt disappeared, though vehicles could still manage it for a stretch, and then the packed-earth road gradually narrowed into a bridle trail, a path fit only for pack animals and for men walking on foot and, probably, although it would be hard to say why, in silence.

To the right as you went along the path, the fields, at times marked off by low, mortarless stone walls or large shrubs and brambles, and at others by rows of black poplars or elm trees struggling to recover from Dutch elm disease, stretched as far as the river; on the left, as if the extraordinary fertility of the other side of the road had wanted to display there its exact opposite, isolated sections of dry hills populated by thyme, gorse, and Spanish lavender jutted up, the path the only break between them. The road skirted those hills, at first along the flanks of the slopes and mud-filled gullies, and soon thereafter, somewhere around three-quarters of the way to the field, you would come to the edge of an imposing, rocky promontory known as Pedralén. There, high up in one of the hollows of the immense, sheer-faced crag, Egyptian vultures—the smallest of their kind and yet just as impressive as the rest—had been building their nests ever since he could remember.

Now, on his return, he noted how on many summer days there were cars parked on the other side of the river, in a few places where the highway opened out, and their passengers, equipped with binoculars, spent their leisure time watching them, observing every little detail as they soared and glided on wings extended and curved slightly to the rear, as if wanting to embrace all that immensity. They contemplated with delight the chicks in the nests, the females, and the males, also, sitting on the eggs; they watched their flights, solitary or in pairs, or they waited hours and hours, with the true patience of naturalists, for them to return from their long absences in search of carrion.

It would have been easy for a typical, run-of-the-mill person, though not at all for an expert or anyone willing to pay a little attention, to have mistaken an Egyptian vulture at first glance for a stork, a scavenger that devours carcasses for the avian symbol of fertility and good omens. Misperceptions like that always seemed odd, even shocking, he thought to himself, but that's the way it was, that's the way things are even when they aren't.

Certainly when they're in the air, at first glance the most noticeable thing is the lightness, or even the whiteness, of the Egyptian vulture's feathers, in slight contrast to the black tips of its wings, but the vulture's neck and feet, for anyone who focuses on them for even a brief moment, are in fact much shorter and less slender than a stork's.

Díaz Carrión, Felipe Díaz Carrión, knew from an early age, from the first times his father, may he rest in peace, took him along on the road to the field, that Egyptian vultures were the first vultures to arrive on the scene wherever there was carrion. Generally they are quiet and quick, his father told him, impressing him to the point of awe, quieter and quicker than anyone else, and despite their large size, they don't make the type of dramatic commotion other vultures do, so sometimes they go unnoticed even though they're always there from the beginning, going about their business. What happens, he would tell him, is that in spite of being the first to arrive—at times one might say even to the point of getting to the victim while it's still in its death throes—what with that very long, thin, yellow beak they have, its black tip curved delicately into a hook, they can only slurp down the soft parts of carcasses; the soft parts, his father would repeat, and he would later repeat to himself, often recalling it even when he was probably thinking about other things—the soft parts, like entrails and, especially, eyes and tongues.

So the Egyptian vulture—his father would go on explaining—needs the larger vultures, the black vulture and the griffon vulture and the bearded vulture

18

with its frightening, black wings and huge beak that
strikes terror in you even from afar, to tear open and
rip apart the carcasses beforehand, so that they, as if
by mutual agreement, can then enjoy the victims' soft
remains. Without the large scavengers, he would say,
without those great, black, repulsive beasts, they would
be nothing; they would gradually go extinct or lead a
miserable, meaningless life.

It's the age-old agreement among the shrewd, Felipe,
my boy—he would say, regardless of how much he was
actually understanding him—it's the calculus of the
cunning, the prerogative of brutality, it's the divvying up
of plunder, a point of access to the spoils for those who,
for whatever reason, call the shots, no matter how much
they complain or may even make their complaints the
most brutal part of that calculus, he would conclude, his
eyes always looking at the road with a gaze he was never
able to understand until his own became the same.

Then he would grow silent, and they would walk
side by side in silence, though each of them would talk
or daydream a great deal to himself; he would imagine
himself, for example, stretched peacefully out in the
grass on the steep banks by the river, or even in his
bed in his room, which looked out onto the patio with
the old cherry tree, and suddenly an enormous black
vulture pouncing on him, suffocating him with its great
wings or ripping him apart, or maybe just the opposite,
an Egyptian vulture he had at first glance mistaken for
a stork and even gotten to the point of petting, and it
would devour his tongue and his eyes and slurp up his
brain and his guts.

Many years later, Felipe Díaz Carrión would think about the circumstance of the Egyptian vulture, the mutual agreement among scavengers, the unspoken arrangement, instinctive and at the same time, despite all the painful peckings they may exchange, highly rational, that exists between those huge, black vultures, with their terrifyingly huge wingspan, even bigger than an eagle's, always lying in wait with their talons and their sharp beaks, and the elegant, white Egyptian vulture you could almost mistake for a stork and yet it devours your entrails and leaves you with no eyes, and no tongue.

3

Beneath the imposing crag they called Pedralén, on the river side of the road—on the right as you went toward the field—and directly beneath the highest point of that immense rock, there now stood a modest cross soberly hewn from stone, which had been erected in the years he hadn't been there. It measured a bit more than three feet high and was perched on a footing made of the same stone, on which several names had been chiseled. And further on, beyond the cross and Pedralén's rocky ravine, where the Egyptian vulture kept its nest from mid-February well into August, it was, finally, only a short trip to the field.

The road curved around two more times still at the base of the ridge, and on the side by the river's edge, covering the entire, fertile plain that separated it from the banks, there grew in rows a stand of black poplars whose leaves would whisper when the wind blew through them and always kept him company, like a welcome when he arrived and a farewell when he left, and which spread its coolness right up to the path, flanked with its elder, its bisnaga, and its danewort, that ended on the right, some fifty yards from the riverbed, at his modest work shed. In total, from the great, sturdy door with the bronze knocker at his house on the outskirts of the village to the little door of gray, rotten wood, which was never varnished and never taken care of, it could not have been much more than around two and a half miles, which Felipe Díaz Carrión, like his father and grandfather before him—both of them named Felipe Díaz, too—would negotiate in about three-quarters of an hour at a brisk but leisurely pace.

For many years, throughout his childhood and part of his adulthood, before or after completing his work at the village printshop, at dawn or at dusk or even on weekends, Felipe Díaz Carrión had taken that road on foot or by burro. To him, it was much more than a mere road or a mere connection between two points. It was a connection, unquestionably, but it connected a lot more than just two points, a lot more than a point of departure and a point of arrival, his house on the outskirts of the village and the work shed in the field, or the other way around; it connected his inner spirit—his soul, he would sometimes say—to the world, and perhaps even to something much greater or lesser than either.

That road was his strength, his life's mettle, it was the very nature of his inclination toward the world, and also his disappearance from it. It was also his entire understanding, as if he had gradually been forging his experience of life and his relationships to people and things almost entirely on that path, on that continuous coming and going and coming back and going again, ruminating on what he saw and seeing what he was ruminating about, on that slow and measured placing and settling of things, seeing the common in the different and seeing things that were the same differently, coming to accept the slings and sorrows of life by allowing the positive to reign, moving beyond his personal emptinesses and solitudes while hearing the echo of his footsteps and the impenetrable sound of the wind in the leaves of the poplar trees, which he interpreted differently depending on the day and the light and the season, and from that, from all of that, he might have been able—without ever knowing how, and with much greater success than from the reading he had with great effort been doing on his own or from the dealings he had kept up with people, also with great effort—to attain a sort of quiet, inextricable, magma-like power and an odd, taciturn, melancholic, wise calmness, both in turn patiently interwoven around the eternal enigmas of life and the signposts, no less enigmatic but forever changing, of time.

4

But one day, just after he broke the long family line of Felipes by naming his son, who had just turned a brilliant eight, Juanjo—Juan José Díaz García—the local printshop he had worked at for what you might call half a lifetime went belly-up. Times had changed, and the old processes of traditional presses had suddenly become as antiquated in the face of new technologies as plows and threshers had not long before. From one day to the next, he found himself without a job, and the field alone was not enough; he tried to find other work in the village or one of the surrounding towns, at first still in his field of graphic arts, and afterward even in just anything, but it was all useless—temporary jobs or piecework, small things here and there, nothing at all. It was as if all the capital and all the projects and all the connections and preferential treatment had moved off elsewhere, and people had no choice but to follow them.

For a while, to try to stave off what increasingly seemed inevitable, he even tried working as a day hand in others' fields while intensifying and rationalizing the cultivation of his own, spending hours there, day in, day out. But it wasn't enough. They had enough to eat, sure, they didn't want for food, but they had nothing more than that. For his wife, Asun, not a single new dress, for their son, not a single treat, no relief whatsoever, and, more than anything, no hint of better days ahead.

It was a time when many young people and even some not-so-young people emigrated from the area to large cities and industrial zones, to Barcelona or Madrid, to Zaragoza or the industrial towns and centers in the north, and that's just the ones who didn't cross the Pyrenees or even the Atlantic. Those cities and regions seemed to have made off with all the wealth and activity in the country, with all the advantages and incentives, and more than anything else, they seemed to hold an absolute monopoly on the future. There wasn't a night when Asun didn't greet his return with the same little song and dance. Let's go, Felipe, let's go where there's more potential, where there's more of everything; do it for your son. That's how it always ended—do it for your son. And so he did. One day, at dawn— the countryside and the streets were still damp from a storm the evening before—they gathered together everything they could fit into a pair of big suitcases and a few bags and they closed, for who knew how long, the great, sturdy door, with its bronze knocker, of their house on the outskirts of the village. They went north, which was, in the end, the place closest to hand, to one of the large, industrial towns in one of the green, misty lowlands of Guipúzcoa.

There, after a while, following a few months spent working construction, he finally got a steady job in a chemical factory, and it wasn't long before they began making mortgage payments on a place that was small compared to the one in his hometown but adequate, located in one of the six identical, giant apartment buildings that had just been built on the outskirts of town, on the very route to the factory itself. From the dining room window, which faced the street, as opposed to the other rooms, which looked out onto an inner courtyard, there was a nice view, to the point that you could see a good stretch of the highway whose shoulder he walked along each day to get to work.

He rose at dawn, just like in his hometown, downed his coffee, and sometimes a second one, and grabbed the sandwich Asunción had made for him, then he took off walking down the highway for what amounted to a bit more than half an hour, to the factory's high, black fence capped by spearheads in the shape of halberds. He would slowly leave behind, one by one, an old, dismal metalworks from which, even in the early morning hours, there issued an incomprehensible screeching; a tire retread shop whose premises he felt from the very beginning were completely disproportionate, with an attached lot, beyond a blackened, stucco wall, where he could see loads of large truck tires and little car tires all piled up, and which sometimes emitted a stench of burning rubber—it stank to high heaven, he would say, even though what he breathed inside the factory most days was no better—and a high-roofed hangar of some sort that went on forever, with no windows or any openings on that side at all, graffitied over with a labyrinth of signs, symbols, and initials he would slowly begin to decipher. Farther on, the only things he would pass were an automobile dealership, a warehouse for who knows what, and a gas station whose lot was jammed at specific times of day with huge trucks, as a result, from what he'd heard, of the more than satisfactory restaurant it had. Except for a few buildings for rent and one highway interchange, that was the last thing he had to pass before he got to the factory.

Cars zoomed by, whipping up the air beside him, replacing it with fumes he had a hard time getting used to breathing, while the trucks seemed as if they were going to tip him over, swallowing him up in the great pockets of emptiness they created in their wake. In the early morning, as well as in winter when he was going back home in the dark, the combination of their headlights would illuminate him intermittently, in flashes, and there were always some who honked at him or sped close past him, so he usually kept as far onto the shoulder as he could.

This is what you've become, he would think, a man on the side of a road, a man on the shoulder of a road, that's what you've become; your road isn't really a road anymore, it's the shoulder of a road, a margin, a bank, but it's not even a riverbank, it's the bank bordering this highway. And he would look at the ground, he would look at his steps on the asphalt or on the packed earth, he would look at the spent cigarette butts and the discarded soda cans, some of them squashed flat as a sheet of paper and others just dented or twisted but in any case tossed aside, thrown away, used up and then scorned, like the plastic bags and wrappers and junk or scrap metal you could see here and there among the filthy clumps of sod, among the weeds that grew unaccountably out of the cracks in the cement like some form of unrecognizable plant life reminiscent of factory runoff, like a kind of cross between vegetation and industrial output.

But the worst stretch for him, the one that seemed the longest, was the giant, windowless wall of that interminable, graffitied hangar, which, although he didn't know why, made him feel so helpless, or, paradoxically, so exposed, and then also later on when he would cross the gravel of the gas station's expansive lot, making his way through the parked trucks. As he walked among those mastodons, with the soles of his feet unstable and unbalanced on the pebbles, he felt not only small and spiritless, as if he were a tiny, disposable thing, but also something akin to an inexplicable auger of anxiety in his stomach.

5

But the years, now marked by the rhythm of that commute, which had gradually become as familiar as his old road to the field, were passing comfortably. Asun, his wife, after a difficult adjustment period, seemed to be feeling more and more at home as time went on, and their son—their elder son, because a year after they moved there, they'd had another one, and with this one he had insisted, perhaps for reasons of nostalgia, on naming him Felipe—was well into his teenage years and had begun not only to go out with his posse of friends but to be out with them at what you might call every waking hour, in fact. To him, there was nothing as important as his posse, and no household routine or opinion, or, in any case, not his father's, held the least value for him compared to those his friends would spout.

If once in a while it happened that he saw his son in their company—all of them as a rule in their coats or black leather jackets, their expressions looking unfriendly or as if they were owed something and would never be paid back, or never fully—the boy would of course act like he hadn't seen him or hadn't recognized him. He would turn his back on him or look off in a different direction, and in that other direction he would see that he was being increasingly barred from butting in with his paternal hoe to try to get rid of any weeds or secure any property markers.

Only when he was out with the pleasant-looking, young priest, the one with the pale complexion and a refined but friendly manner about him, or with the town councilman who was also the principal of a neighborhood school, whose friendliness, truth be told, was equally striking, did he deem it worth his trouble to say hello or even come over to him. It was clear he wanted to show off these friendships to his father, or show him who he was associating with, and he, in turn, would readily agree to exchange a few words with them, despite the fact that there was something about them, their carefulness itself, perhaps, their very amiability, from which he was nonetheless unable to separate a feeling of mistrust or detached condescension toward him that made him feel lesser or exposed, out of place, you might say, which made him even more confused than ever and prompted him to say to himself, perhaps with a bit of deep-seated exaggeration, that in spite of all, he almost preferred those casting the baleful eyes and wearing the black leather jackets. At least with them, he thought, no one was trying to put something over on you. So he would see his son, he would see his baleful eyes before he turned his back on him when he was with those casting their own baleful eyes, and then he would see his gleaming gaze, like a stork's, when he would come over to him with the councilman or the little, pale-faced priest, but he couldn't help but see him growing ever further apart, becoming even more of a stranger, flying far, far away in baffling and surely seductive circles he himself would never be able to enter.

It was true that Juanjo not only didn't turn out to be much of a student but rather that at the first opportunity, or, to be more precise, right after they moved there, began to disparage academic instruction and all those who took their studies seriously—they're just a bunch of losers, he would say—and an increasingly sour, anti-social attitude, which might, of course, be normal for a teenager but already showed signs of being anything but temporary here, had gradually and inexorably begun to dominate him. There would be days when he wouldn't see him; he would come home—if he came home at all—very late at night, sometimes even when he was getting up and rushing to make his coffee before quickly grabbing his sandwich and leaving without wasting a minute, to wend his way to the factory. But no one could get through to him; if he ever tried to reprimand him for some reason or criticize him for something even slightly, not to mention if he ever told him off, he would waste no time in raising his voice with such anger and expressing such rage on his face, often with his mother's support and understanding, that he would fall into a state of sheepish, impotent distress. So he slowly got used to putting up with his presence—just as one puts up with a hailstorm, he said to himself—and to hoping that by completely giving up any and all criticism of him, it might all clear itself up and he might eventually get his head screwed on right.

In the meantime, he had adapted well to factory life, to the various shifts, and even to the work itself, as well as to the trip to and from his neighborhood, which he seemed to make ever more acceptingly. In the morning, most of the time, he would wrap his sandwich in a sheet from one of the newspapers his son would bring home and then always leave around— on occasion flauntingly, he thought—and sometimes later on, during the lunch break, when he was eating it somewhere away from everyone else so he wouldn't have to exchange a lot of idiotic, from his point of view, small talk with his coworkers—or put up with the complaints of those who, even though they may have good reason for it, never stop complaining about this or that or, more often than not the other thing— he would pass the time reading quietly, focusing, as his father had taught him from the time he was a small boy, on the words that said things and the ones that didn't. Words are like birdsongs, he would explain; each person expresses themselves in their own way, just as each bird sings in its own way, and just as with birdsong, you know by their words who's talking and what they're up to.

Sometimes he would read news about crimes— attacks, the newspaper would say, violence, groups of people who murdered other groups of people, executed them, he had read, eliminated them, or kidnapped them, or put bombs under their cars or along the roadside—half-articles that began on a previous page or continued on a following one that he didn't have there with him, or maybe fragments of articles or incomplete reports, which he read as fully as he could and hardly ever spoke about with anyone else.

But if he was only gradually getting used to the changes, his wife, Asun, Asunción García Bellido, especially now that their younger son was getting older, had been putting together a group of friends and finding ways to keep busy and seemed to have become perfectly acclimated or, as she put it, integrated. It was crystal clear that she was becoming more and more decisive, more sure of what she was doing and, especially, of what she was saying, even to the point, in his humble opinion, of becoming a bit arrogant. But even though it was true that the sweet, loving personality she'd had up to recently had been changing and that she had acquired manners that were not only brusque but disrespectful and volatile in a way he hadn't seen in her previously, he thought it must have something to do with her getting older, with her struggle for life and to keep moving forward, with her satisfaction, even, at having succeeded in that, and that one didn't always need to be the same in life and maybe what you were before wasn't necessarily better. Just the opposite, in fact. Change enriches your life, it wakes you up, it motivates you; to see that, you just had to look at her—determined, full of energy and curiosity. What had happened was basically that the strong and decisive personality that hadn't had any opportunity or avenue to develop in her youth had blossomed there. They were different times—even though not so many years had passed, if you really looked at it—and different circumstances.

Without a doubt, now it was she who called the shots in the house, and a lot of the time it was a pleasure to listen to what she had to say; it was as if she had come out of her shell, as if she had bid goodbye to all prior inhibition or shyness, to all timidity, and she even gave the impression of having studied, or at least of having learned, a never-ending grab bag of words and phrases which she would spit out in rapid fire with an astonishing degree of self-assurance that never ceased to amaze him. She would speak more and more frequently, just as their elder son did, for that matter, about all the attacks—or actions, which is the way their son would put it—against people whose human dignity, he'd noted, they always seemed, though he could never figure out or understand why, to have negated from the outset, with a feeling of rancor and malevolence that was incomprehensible to him despite the explanations both of them insisted on giving him. It seems to me that neither of you has any idea what you're talking about, he would sometimes shrug, eventually lowering his head before beating a slow retreat so as not to have to go on with these disputes that struck him as falling on deaf ears, on deaf ears, he would say, with people who have decided on principle that they don't want to understand.

So it seemed like he was the only one who was having a hard time getting fully acclimated or integrated, as his wife and elder son would say. It wasn't for lack of trying, it's true, and he gave everything he had to convince himself that it had all been for the best, that it was plain they had prospered in an endless variety of ways—you had only to look at his wife—or at least that there had really been no alternative. On Saturdays, and often on Sundays, when Asun would go out with her friends, he would head to a bar on the ground floor of one of the six identical apartment buildings where they lived—the second one on the side nearest the highway, if you were coming from the factory— and there, for better or worse, he would pass the time playing cards with a group of his neighbors. But after a few years, the bar's ownership changed, and along with the change in ownership, there was a change in patronage, and several of his friends, those who like him had come from elsewhere as well as locals, gradually stopped coming. You just don't get it, they would say to him.

The walls of the bar started filling up with flags, photographs of people he didn't recognize, notices for one meeting or another, and slogans similar to the ones crammed and overlapping on the wall of the long hangar he went by, feeling confused and helpless, every day on the way to work. Even the coffee, which was practically the only thing he drank, had changed. He now found it more acidic, and stronger, or maybe it was the milk or the way it was prepared, which, like everything else, seemed to have transformed there from one day to the next. We'll see, he told himself.

But if at first it all seemed strange—the distant and at times almost contemptuous treatment, as if they had no desire to make the least effort to keep certain customers or it didn't matter to them at all whether they came or stopped coming, or even if they suspected that what they really wanted was to get rid of them without a second thought (although he'd kept going—what the heck, after all, we're just talking about a cup of coffee or a beer every once in a while, he would tell himself)—it seemed to him that in an instant, out of a clear, blue sky, they were willing to pay more attention to him. Both the waiter and the rest of the customers, whose sullen expressions he had pretended not to see before, now began to turn to him with sudden familiarity, making jokes about things or referring to facts he feigned knowing about despite the fact that, most of the time, he was actually in the dark, and the rest of the time, well, the truth was that he actually preferred not to know.

That was about the same time his son Juanjo left home. He had found work somewhere else, in France, his wife told him after he hadn't seen him for a few days. It wasn't out of the ordinary that whole days or sometimes even weeks would go by without seeing him, without having what one might call any real contact with him, like having lunch or dinner together, for example, or going out for a walk, but on that occasion, although he didn't really know why, he had a funny feeling that this time was different.

"Work, what kind of work?" he asked his wife.

"Work . . . what do I know, I don't understand all this newfangled business," she answered. "It was about time he went off on his own anyway."

"Well if *you* don't understand . . ." he replied.

Juanjo was twenty-seven years old at that point, Felipe had just turned sixteen, and it was true that it really wasn't too soon for him to leave home, but it seemed to him—and this is how he put it to himself— that for a long time, and it was hard to figure out an exact date, but in any case it was just a few years after they moved, he hadn't had any jurisdiction when it came to his older boy. He had lost him, he had lost control of him long before he left home without feeling the slightest need to say anything to him about it.

One day, one of the last days he saw him stop by the house—it was a Saturday, and it had been a sparkling afternoon—he noticed that he was more self-absorbed and unsociable than usual, which was saying something; it seemed like he was weighed down by some burden— perhaps a romantic disappointment, he thought, or one of those impossible headaches that seem overwhelming to young people but that disappear as easily as a puff of smoke—that was eating away at his insides and he couldn't take it any longer. He asked him what was going on, and he asked him, not without some trepidation, if he could help.

"How are you going to help me, you're just a worthless fucking hayseed," he spat at him in reply, "a worthless hayseed, and one of them, too."

For a few seconds he was caught short, he was totally unable to react, whether this way or that, and at the end of those seconds, and doing his utmost to remain calm and not slap him in the face—which might be what he should in fact have done, he told himself later—he asked who, one of who.

"One of them, who do you think, one of those disgusting, pile-of-shit pieces of scum that don't let us live and have kept us historically oppressed," he rattled off without stopping for breath, glaring at him with an air of arrogant disdain and accusatory resentment he was unable, despite having gotten gradually used to it, to find much of an explanation for, as was the case with so many other things.

"What would you know about being oppressed, much less historically oppressed?" he heard himself answering suddenly under his breath, like someone who has let himself say something he knows is useless, something it would perhaps have been better to have let go unsaid.

And from that moment, from a simple *what would you know* that had come tumbling out of his mouth unbidden and a *historically* he'd repeated back without knowing how or why he'd done it but knowing it had been on purpose, free rein was given to the furious argument that, right from the start, he had been unable to make sense of or know how to frame, especially considering the person to whom he was speaking, or even to know how to extricate himself from, no matter how hard he had been trying, from the instant it had been set in motion, to do just that.

More than an argument, though, more than a proper dispute in which each party, no matter how combative they might feel, still sets up his reasons in opposition to the other person's, his arguments and facts in opposition to the facts and arguments of the other person, what this was, in fact, from the very moment it erupted, was a mere unilateral outburst of hostility, a pure and simple demonstration of rivalry, of a need to project onto this rivalry a contradictory swarming of internal impulses and, in so doing, to find an easy outlet for them, a banal, substitutive escape valve, a categorical, prideful sublimation. It was also, in addition to all that, an increasingly wrathful, violent act of venting on his son's part, by means of which, to the father's increasingly afflicted and alarmed amazement, he continued to fling reproaches and shower blame on him, to toss out accusations and call him bitterly to account, as if he had spent more time than one could bear just waiting for the occasion to present itself, to be able to burst out, but never finding the right reason or moment to do so—the fault of his worthless fucking last name, he yelled, his worthless fucking hometown, his sheeplike submissiveness, and his revolting poverty, his old age, his spinelessness, his inactivity, all day long depressed and playing cards, the fault of his having been born precisely to whom he had been born and having a father who was an absolute nobody, a nothing, and an out-and-out fascist.

"You know something?" the father cut him off cleanly before turning on his heels, his heart in his throat, and going out to walk, without knowing why, along that same road with the metalworks and the tire retread shop and then the giant wall of that huge, overwhelming hangar, and after that the lot at the gas station, chock-full of parked cars and trucks at that hour on a Saturday, which he tried to make his way through as best he could, his insides all tied up in knots, in order to carry on. "You know something? Your father may not know a whole heckuva lot, and he may be just as poor and unimportant as you say, but there's one thing he does know, and it's this: that in this world, some things are fair and some things are unfair; some things are as they should be and some things are complete madness, no matter how you slice them; some things, like in the country, grow healthy and it does you good to see them, but then some things are so puny and so riddled with disease it's as if they brought it on themselves; and some things seem to naturally bring about a general good and other things bring nothing but calamity and atrocity to everyone around them. Some things are true, really and truly true, and some things are no more than hogwash and evil illusions, and some things are lawful and others are unlawful, some are tolerable and others are unequivocally intolerable, like terrorizing, intimidating and offending people, not to mention killing people, killing anyone, for any reason whatsoever. And I also know, no matter how much you might mock me, that some things are truly noble and some things are true, colossal shams, some are worthy and some are filthy and repugnant and worthless, some things are doable and some things impossible and treacherous, and some do good for the majority of people and some, sooner or later, are counterproductive for almost everybody, even for those who prattle on the entire livelong day about them.

"There's a fine line between them, and it's true that at times, rather than a confusing or a changeable line, it's a skittish line, as my father used to say, or as people said he used to say, and sometimes it seems it's in one place and other times it's in another place, and a lot of the time it gives the impression it's neither in the one nor the other, but every thing, just like every field, just like every garden, no matter how big it is, has, in the end, invariably, a dividing line, and there is a limit to everything, and a limit of all limits—You hear me? Do you hear me? Would you do me the blasted favor of listening to me for once in your life?—and if you cross that line, there will most likely be no going back, no matter how much ideological tommyrot you try dishing out or how much immoral lunacy you're willing to put up with, and that line is the life of others, you hear me? It's the life of human beings, which is sacred, even though you might laugh when I use the word, just as you might laugh if I mentioned *honor*, other people's honor and your own honor, and *scruples*, too, scruples about hurting others, and the humiliation of being hurt, but it doesn't matter—other people's honor and scruples about hurting them, as my father, may he rest in peace, used to say, those are the fine lines that give worth to your own freedom and the freedom of others.

"And I also know that one thing is a thing itself, and another, very different thing is the way it's tinkered with and twisted, it's exploitation—and these are your words I'm using, mind; and I know that of course each of us sees and thinks in his own way, but as convinced as someone may be that he is right about something, or in the right about something (and you can always convince yourself of whatever you like and for whatever reason, as your grandfather apparently always used to say, too), that doesn't mean that other people are under any obligation to see and think like him, nor that that person has the right to any such a thing, much less any kind of historical right, as you put it without, I believe, understanding a blessed word, and I know that a person, not to belabor the point, can do whatever he wants, it's true, but not just whatever he feels like, meaning that he can do what he likes, as long as he doesn't bother or intimidate or frighten anybody else, or, of course, lay a single finger on them. Do you understand me, my son?"

With his mouth half open, his upper lip raised slightly at its left corner, his eyes a bit dulled and oddly fixed, and with his chin lifted a touch and his head cocked and tilted to one side, he stood there when he'd finished, staring at him with a look that wasn't merely of surprise or lack of understanding, nor was it of disdain, exactly, or contempt or slandered petulance alone, but all of that at the same time, as well—very especially—as disgust, revulsion, and illimitable, deaf, impotent spite, a deeply insurmountable spite toward someone who, if given the chance, he wouldn't have thought twice about squashing like a bug right then and there.

He'd called him *son*, *my son*, he'd had the audacity to call him *my son* not only after not having called him that for so long but, as if that weren't enough, after this diatribe of his, as direct and devastating as a fist, unchallengeable, in which he'd given him the piece of his mind he should have given him long ago, and on top of all that, after he'd had to stand there hearing him out, and hell if he knew how he'd had the patience to stand there and hear that whole thing out, that repulsive sermonizing that passed for a response out of this self-righteous, small-town yokel, this insignificant, laughable piece of shit who'd had the nerve to unleash this diatribe on him as if he were some small-town priest, a sour, dried-out old schoolmaster who has no idea, who doesn't have a clue about anything, or like some mutt dragging itself along the side of the highway, pleading loudly for some unstoppable higher force to squash him once and for all and remove him already from the face of this earth.

6

Although he saw him at the house from time to time after that dustup, they didn't address more than a few perfunctory words or curt remarks to one another, and when he found out from his wife that he had gone— gone, according to what she said, to France and to work—he felt something akin to relief. You'll regret it soon enough, said one of those friends of his who at other times had also told him that he just didn't get it.

One of the last times he saw him, if not the last time itself—actually it was only a moment as he came out of his bedroom and went through the dining room on his way to the front door—was a Sunday afternoon at the beginning of November, the weather was still pleasant, and everybody, except his wife, had stayed at home in the apartment. He was more sunk in his easy chair than stretched out on it, like on a lot of other Sunday afternoons, when he spent his time waiting for Asun to show up and get their dinner together, and keeping his younger son, Felipe, company; that day, he was focused on the plant collection he kept. His wife spent a lot of afternoons with her friends—or whatever they were—at some association he didn't know a thing about, nor did he want to, and some days, but especially Saturdays and Sundays, she would often get home late, as a rule after the league soccer games that were blasting on television and radio sets all over the neighborhood were over.

One by one, his younger son was laying out on the expanded dining room table, which he had completely taken over, the samples of plants he had collected the previous day. He was placing them between the folds of sheets of newsprint, on top of which, like a press, he then placed several fat volumes of the encyclopedia, and then, taking care to follow the same numbering he had assigned to each of the plants he had placed there to dry, he wrote on little slips of cream-colored paper their common and scientific names, and the place and date he had collected each of them. He wrote with a very careful hand, diligently, with a painstakingness that one might say was oblivious not only to the passage of time that afternoon but also to the fact that he was sitting there in that space, among the garish furniture that was too big for the small size of the room and very uncomfortable and almost impractical, to the point that it seemed to be arguing with whoever was using it. Later, as he contemplated each and every plant as if it were a miracle, he would read aloud the characteristics that described them scientifically, and his face would light up when he saw how much the scientific description and the classified reality coincided, the words he read and the thing he had there, right in front of his eyes.

"They're not women, Einstein, they're just a bunch of friggin' weeds!" his older brother had told him more than once, and he said it to him again that afternoon.

Felipe knew that nothing could make his father happier than inviting him to go out to the hills with him to collect plants. What do you say we go for an excursion this Saturday, he would ask him, and he knew that from the moment he asked, he would be counting the days and making preparations and coming up with ideas for their itinerary. He had gotten ahold of a good number of maps (Army maps!—he would say), which he would pour over at all hours, memorizing the trails and crossings, the altitudes of the different mountains and the names of the different *caseríos*, like someone immersing himself in the syllabus for a major examination in the hope of being useful to his son.

Besides the maps, in order to keep the plants separate from one another and transport them safely back home, they went armed with a hefty bundle of old copies of the newspapers his brother usually bought, and sometimes, when they would sit down to rest or wolf down the lunch or the snack they had prepared for themselves, they would read a page silently, almost furtively, without sharing any of it or talking to one another about what they were reading.

They also took a plant manual with photographs and scientific descriptions of every species, and one of their greatest joys was not only coming upon some new plant they didn't yet have in their herbarium but finding the corresponding plant in the book. That's . . . that's, one would say, wood sage, would you look at that—*Teucrium scorodonia*, the other would rejoin, of the family Lamiaceae—its leaves have elongated petioles, yes, that's right, ovate limbs, either heart-shaped or incurved at the stem, yes, that's right, rough to the touch, with rounded, dentate margins. A real, live *Teucrium scorodonia*, no doubt about it, with its flowers in a spiky cluster, its corollas, yes, a whitish-yellowish color and sticking out quite a lot from the bilabial calyx, and its bracts, just so, small, oval, and much shorter than the leaves. Or wait, look, what do you know, another ragwort, but it's not a groundsel, not a *Senecio vulgaris*, it's a *Senecio erucifolius*, which I don't think we have. It says very clearly here: Its supplementary bracts are found in a cluster of between four and eight at the base of the flower itself, like this one; so, more and longer bracts than in the other *Senecios* we have.

"And this one," his son asked him one day with unusual surprise when confronted with the fetid odor and viscous feel of a plant whose leaves were cloven deeply into two lobes at the tip, "what would this one be?"

The flower's corolla, pale yellow but scored with many, many sinews of an enigmatic purple, the same color that darkened the gorge from which they'd just emerged, produced in him, too, a disquieting, disagreeable sensation, and he didn't know if it came from fascination or repulsion, or perhaps both at the same time.

"That's one I've known for a long time; they grow, or at least they used to, if you knew where to look, on the road that went out to the field back home, too. It's henbane, look it up in the index and you'll see."

"I'm not sure if it's pretty, or really pretty, or actually really ugly, only that it really catches your eye; boy, does it catch your eye."

To see something, the father or the son thought, or they might have thought, to see a plant, for example, or a flower, and give it a name, to see it there among so many other identical or similar or perhaps completely different or even opposite things and try to identify it, to find some connection to something you've noticed other times or even to something that's been discerned once and for all, to see something and take note of it, so as not to forget, to see it and formulate a hypothesis about what you've seen and then later confirm it or reject it and thus to advance step by step and with open eyes; to see and then to verify what you've seen, to accept it, to act in accordance. To discover such a connection produced in them a strange delight, to corroborate some correspondence, to assign a name, to see that between words and things there is at times no friction, no entrapment, no argument but instead a lengthening of your reach, an expansion of your vision, independent of however repulsive or fascinating or insipid it may all appear at first glance. Every time they would figure out the name of a plant, it seemed to them the world opened up, that it broadened, that it was more capacious, that it became more detailed and grew both within them and outside of themselves. Perhaps joy—they would say to themselves, or they might think— was just a type of opening up, and hatred, conversely, was a narrowing, a strangulation of the world.

His younger son was reading on that same, still-benign November afternoon about the properties of the henbane they had collected weeks earlier—the roots, his father said to him, the roots are almost always the most narcotic part—when suddenly the door to the older brother's room, which he generally kept sealed tight, opened, and he came out with a heavy-looking bag and made for the front door. From his chair at the far end of the dining room, next to the window, the father noticed that as soon as the bedroom door opened, the two boys exchanged a fleeting look, as if each of them knew what the other was thinking.

"They're not women, Einstein, you stupid little brat, they're just a bunch of friggin' weeds!" he said to him suddenly, for the umpteenth time, as he went by, giving him a poke in the back of the neck and then a slap on the cheek that knocked off his glasses.

Without thinking, without even a split second of time between the slap he'd gotten and his immediate, unprecedented reaction, Felipe threw himself at his brother's throat like a wildcat, knocking him to the ground with a crash that was amplified by the narrowness of the hallway. He hadn't answered back, he hadn't tried to stand up for himself this time with any arguments or demands, nor had he spoken one word of subservience, of forbearance, of defense, or of anything else, but instead, impelled by a strength his older brother didn't realize and didn't even suspect existed, as if it had been brewing and bubbling inside him for ages, waiting for just the right moment when his cup of patience, long since filled to brimming, would finally overflow, he grabbed him by the neck with everything he had and a headlock so tight it was as if he wanted to strangle him, and he flung him around, banging him against the floor and the wall, while his brother, stupefied at the surprise and his astonishing strength, seemed more concerned with not letting go of his bag than with fighting back with the only free hand left to him in his position. But he didn't; at that point not only did he not defend himself, he didn't fight back. Maybe it was the shock—who the hell would have thought it from a wimpy, milquetoast little shit like that, he said a few days later—or maybe it was the fact that he couldn't make use of his other hand, or maybe, more likely, it was his brother's unexpected, at long last resolved strength, but he didn't defend himself or even seem very surprised when his father immediately came to his aid—let him alone, Felipe, let him alone, boy, come on, for my sake, he said, trying to separate them—instead, he just seemed glad not to have dropped his bag, and then he turned around after opening the front door to leave and said in a loud, clear voice, with a look it didn't take his father long to recognize, that if he ever came across the little shithead again, he just might not live to tell the tale.

You just might not live to tell the tale, people were in the habit of saying that—and other people were in the habit of hearing it—as though it were the most natural thing in the world, or just wait, you'll be sorry, or you're gonna get it, think about what you're doing, I'm not gonna tell you your business, you wouldn't want to end up regretting anything later on, you wouldn't want any unpleasant surprises. Or we'll run into each other sometime soon, kid, don't you worry, this is a really small town and we all know each other here, just you watch yourself, or we'll take care of you soon enough, we know where you live, which car is yours, where you take your son, what time you pick him up, and if one day something happens to you or someone gives you what you've got coming, well, don't come complaining to me, you know best, don't say I didn't warn you. The entire linguistic topography of threats and intimidation encapsulated in expressions—preceded by silences, gestures, and looks—that people had to take in stride, as if living with threats were just as completely normal as the idea that there might be rain one day instead of sun, and it was that more than anything else, more than wealth or age or sex or worth or career, that separated people there into two groups: the people who proffered such expressions with varying degrees of bravado or conviction, and real-life consequences, and the more scattered, defenseless, vulnerable group of people who stood on the receiving end of them with varying degrees of composure—and varying degrees of fear—and then had to face those consequences.

7

The following Sunday, after having watched a television documentary on animals with his son Felipe, he got up the energy to go to the bar on the ground floor of one of those apartment buildings that were all identical to his. He seemed to notice a colder distance in the customers again, but they must all simply be wrapped up in their own musings, he said to himself in a style of a language he practically dared not use any more. After having said hello as he came in, without getting the least response, he ordered a coffee, took off his jacket, and placed it on the back of a chair across from the one he had chosen to sit in.

At a table in the back, about five or six yards away, four people were playing cards, surrounded by several onlookers and speaking in whispers, and though he couldn't have said why, it seemed to him that he was the subject of their comments. Here's your coffee, the owner barked, slamming it down on the bar so hard that it spilled over and flooded the saucer. He got up—the whispering seemed to intensify—and went to retrieve his coffee. There was almost more on the saucer than in the cup, so he picked it up and held it there a moment, letting the drops fall off, and then he took it to the table without the saucer. Careful you don't muck up my table and make it so I gotta spend the whole day cleaning it, he heard a loud voice say. The whole day cleaning shit up, agreed one of the patrons at the bar, while a few other people nodded disdainfully, the whole goddamned day clearing shit out of the way, that's what you gotta do.

He had already grabbed a couple of paper napkins and put them under the cup, and now, as he drank what was left of the coffee, without any sugar so as not to stir up any fuss—the paper packet had been soaked by the spilled liquid—he sat and watched the soccer game being shown on television, but with little interest. A white ball—he couldn't quite understand why it seemed so immaculate to him in its roundness—went from one pair of cleats to another, from one player to another, from one half of the field to the other. They intercepted it from one another, they negotiated with it a bit, they started running after it, and they fell to the ground—or dove onto it—howling in pain in a way that sometimes seemed absurd to him. Why were they howling so much, he would wonder to himself. On the chair across from him, his old jacket on the seat back made for an odd companion, loyal, welcoming. He looked at it—most likely remembering or imagining something or other—and it was as if he were actually engaged in a silent dialogue with it.

When he went to pay for the coffee, he didn't have any change, and because it seemed too small a thing to pay for with the one bill he had, he treated two of the regulars to another of whatever it was they were drinking, even though neither of them—his memory on this point was clear—had responded at all to his greeting when he had come in. Without taking his eyes off his impromptu companions, in whose grins he immediately detected a sneer of sarcasm, he spotted the change from his payment, which was five times more than the price of the drinks, being stuffed by the hand of the owner—whose smile would most likely, if he'd been able to catch more than the final second of it, have matched that of his companions—into a sort of collection box for some prisoners.

"You want us to put this in here, right?" the owner said to him with a slow sneer (that *right* was the final, sarcastic flourish with which the owner punctuated his smile) before he turned away from him in silence, grabbed his jacket from the back of the chair—come on, let's get out of here, he would have liked to have said to it—and left the place for the last time.

A year or thereabouts after this incident, which led him to spend even more time at home, in his chair next to the window in a dining room overly packed with furniture so garish it seemed to be arguing with whoever was using it, the main partner at the company he worked for, an economist with whom he'd exchanged little more than a few polite words, was kidnapped by the organization for whose prisoners he had paid his pence that Sunday. He was leaving his office, his workday finished, to go out and get into his car, which, like always, he'd left in the same old parking space in the factory lot, when two hooded men, who appeared in a flash from out of nowhere, it seemed at first, stuck a pistol at him and took him to a location whose whereabouts remained unknown for almost a year.

When he found out about it, what immediately flashed through his mind, like a bolt of lightning from a looming storm, was the fact that his son had asked him one day, months before their final argument, if he could accompany him to the factory some time when he had his night shift. He'd happily agreed, interpreting this at first glance as a sort of rapprochement or, who knew, perhaps even his son sounding out the possibility of a job. But once there—they had followed the usual route along the shoulder of the road, saying nothing almost the entire time, he waiting for his son to say something to him—and after having offered an offhand hello to this businessman as he, having finished his workday, got into the car he always left in the same parking space next to the entrance, he remembered that he'd mentioned to his son that this was the owner, or half-owner, he believed he'd said. And you go all docile and rush to greet him, huh, had been his response.

Now he realized that it hadn't escaped him at the time how he'd watched him and followed all his movements, how he'd taken in his surroundings without missing the minutest of details or answering with anything more than monosyllabic coolness to the effusiveness with which he showed him one thing or another, his work area, or the different manufacturing processes. Just like in the country, he told him, happy to get the chance to open up to his son, I always try to understand the whole process, to not be satisfied with my small part, which is always the same, but to survey the entire operation and see the final result as something I fully comprehend. And I realize this will seem ridiculous to you, but it makes me feel less alone.

A lot of times, he went on, in the full realization of how ridiculous it all must be sounding to his son, I even stay for a while after my shift is over to see all of it and ask other people questions. Understanding, although not necessarily participating, because that's apparently expecting too much in certain circumstances, makes you feel less rootless, more involved in what you're doing, even if all you're doing is making chemical products. If you don't, you're just allowing inertia to eat you up, you succumb to sloth and monotony and emptiness, or even aggressiveness. And then, since you're not doing well, what pisses you off is that the next guy isn't even worse off, he told him.

What pisses you off, he said, what pisses you off is that the next guy isn't even more pissed off than you, he hammered home, even though that wasn't one of his own expressions, but in an attempt to maybe bring himself closer to his son, in a timid, ridiculous way to try to ingratiate himself to him somehow. But he quickly realized he had made it worse, that the words seemed strange coming from his mouth, as if he weren't pronouncing them exactly right or had given them the wrong tone or degree of effusiveness. He knew that if he had looked his son full in the face at that point, he would have seen in his eyes a narrowed expression of pity mixed with the usual disgust and animosity with which he felt he was normally looked at, and so he didn't do it. Deep down, he had enjoyed telling him those things.

8

He accompanied him to the factory on other occasions, always at the same time of day, never bothering anymore to ask beforehand if he could come along, as if he'd actually taken the time to learn when he was on the night shift and when he wasn't, and even to learn some of the things he had shown to him; and then he also saw him from time to time when he left work, not so much as if he had been waiting for him, although he pretended to be, but as if his leaving work had seemed in fact premature or he had interrupted him in some unrelated activity. But he didn't think it was especially important until the news of the owner's kidnapping, and in the end, even though he couldn't help suspecting that something fishy was going on, it made him feel good, flattered even, to see his son there, whatever the reason and however he glared at him.

From the first weeks after the kidnapping, however—and he didn't really understand why, nor did he need to, he told himself, whether it was that he was trying to rid himself of a niggling suspicion, or perhaps simply for the sake of decency, for the sake of pure decency, which is the answer he gave anyone who asked him, or more like reproached him, about it—he began to head every day at the exact same time to the town square with others of his coworkers in order to silently call for the business man's release. They went after completing their workday, just about the time of day he had been kidnapped, and they gathered in silence in front of the town hall, holding up a banner with large letters against a white background calling for the man's immediate release. There weren't many of them, some of them weren't so young anymore, and they didn't even have all that much confidence in the effectiveness of their gesture, but they stuck it out, standing there together steadfastly for half an hour, even while some people insulted them as if they were asking for something evil.

As the months passed, some of them, having become the objects of insults and intimidation of varying degrees of seriousness—you wouldn't want to end up regretting this, they would say to them, or running into any trouble, I guess we're just gonna have to wait and see, because more than one of you is really gonna get it, and murderers, too, lousy fucking murderers, and traitors, and above all fascists, lousy fucking fascists—had to gradually stop coming, no matter how unwillingly. I have little kids, they would say by way of excuse, or this is getting us nowhere, or there's nothing we can do, and he would pat them on the shoulder and say goodbye with the same calm, melancholic smile as if he were seeing something then that he had been seeing ever since his days spent walking his hometown road many years before.

But without ever making any actual decision or, to be honest, even thinking about it, without mulling it over or weighing it up in his mind or taking into account anything that wasn't what he would call, with words that were most likely a bit grand for him, the absolutely unrenounceable, and giving no excuse whatsoever, he persevered there, as trees and plants persevere, and sometimes, though only sometimes, some people, too. Day after day, no matter the weather, which was pleasant at first but increasingly mired in the inclemency of winter, huddled under an umbrella or sheathed in his greatcoat, and no matter how intense the insults, the disdain, and the lack of understanding became, how widespread the disregard, perhaps more than anything else, that they elicited, he seemed to continue standing there steadfastly in order to remind anyone who cared to listen that some things are fair and some things are unfair; that some things are as they should be and some things are complete madness, no matter which way you slice them; that some things bring about good, even a general good, and other things bring nothing but calamity and atrocity; that some things are true, really and truly true, and not mere acts of exploitation or opportunistic manipulation, and other things are no more than illusions or empty, poisonous hogwash; and some things are lawful and others are clearly unlawful; some things are tolerable and other things are intolerable in every way, like terrorizing, intimidating and offending people, and of course killing people, killing or kidnapping anyone, for any reason whatsoever. And if you refuse to remember that and to keep it in mind in all of your actions, then you are renouncing the unrenounceable, that which makes men deserving of being called men and living among men and makes them capable of truly noble things instead of true, colossal shams, of genuinely free things and not just arrogantly or despicably servile things that sooner or later become counterproductive for everyone. And if it is indeed true that the line of demarcation between them can sometimes be not just confusing and changeable but even skittish, and sometimes it seems it's in one place and other times it's in another place, and a lot of the time it gives the impression that it's neither in the one nor the other, it is also unquestionable that in the end, each and every thing has its dividing line, and for everything there is a limit, and a limit of all limits, the type of limit that if you go beyond it, there will most likely be no going back, no matter what you say or don't say, and that line is the life and safety of others.

His sullen, taciturn profile, his wide, full face, his uncommonly long, thick mustache, more white now than anything else, the wrinkles that furrowed his brow from one side to the other, the few lone hairs on his head—as Asunción always said, ironically, because it seemed he hadn't lost a single hair, and at his age, too— had gradually become a kind of unspoken reference point for that small handful of people who, almost without meaning to, had decided to let their silence be heard, so to speak, in the face of the uproar of anger and the clamor of rhetoric.

But one night, when he returned home after a stint in the square and a beer he had had afterward with a few of the others—Asun wasn't home yet—he was met with a black, plastic bag, like the ones you use to throw out the trash, tied with a knot to the door handle. He found another one the following week, and two weeks later, a dead black cat on the doormat; have it your way, a note said. And a month later, one day after his son Felipe had come home from school so full of cuts and bruises that they'd had to take him to the hospital—it was nothing, he said, some stupid argument that escalated badly—he had barely opened the door to his building when suddenly, without his even having the time to turn on the entryway light, he felt himself being brutally grabbed by two individuals who pushed him into a corner of the vestibule and there, without saying a single word, delivered three or four quick punches to his stomach, knocking him to the ground. As he writhed on the tiled floor—his mouth agape, he gasped for breath, inhaling the filth of the tiles, and his eyes translated the odd angle of light coming in from the street through the glass door and falling across the floor into pain—a deluge of stomping that seemed never-ending, of kicks to his ribs and kidneys and his chest and legs, two or three even finding their way to his face, rained down on him almost before he could understand any of it. And you know who you have to thank that this is as far as it's gone, you fucking traitor, he heard, or he thought he heard, right before seeing their sneakers disappear with the same grim haste with which they had appeared.

In total it might only have been a few minutes, perhaps just a few seconds, nothing in comparison to how long it took him to get up afterward—a neighbor came in with his wife, turned on the light, and, seeing him laid out and bloodied on the floor, they both averted their eyes and went past him as if he didn't exist—and move little by little, bleeding, his body completely shattered, as if life itself might slip away each time he made a movement, back to the elevator door, more dragging himself than walking.

The following week, with unflappable gravity, with something also unmistakably sunny in his demeanor, something akin to happiness, a serene, stubborn happiness radiating from his eyes, he stood as a photojournalist snapped another shot of his sullen profile and thick mustache, and the wrinkles that furrowed his brow from one side to the other of his forehead, on which you could now see the remnants of some sort of laceration of major proportions, behind the banner on which, with large, simple letters on a white background, they continued to demand freedom, and surely not for that one man alone.

9

Almost a year after the industrialist's kidnapping, in a carefully designed operation into which there went several long, patient months of meticulousness and perseverance, the police found the hole in which he had been held captive for just under a year, like one of the living dead. Not the filthiest of dungeons of times past or even the soulless, systematic annihilations in the concentration and extermination camps of our most arrogant century—at least there those poor people were able, for whatever it's worth, to see daylight and a human face, he told himself—were, in the end, what you might call much worse, he thought in stupefaction upon reading the details in that day's newspaper of the pit where that man—and he always called him *that man*, and nothing else—had survived, day after day and hour after hour, until he'd tallied up almost a year of complete isolation.

With no other source of light than a single bulb, permanently lit, day and night, and space enough only to barely spread his two arms and take one, two, three, four, and maybe five little steps in any one direction, with no other air than the dank, rancid stench of the stagnancy therein, and no other connection with the world than the sound, a few times a day, of footsteps, and then afterward, not always immediately but always excitedly, from the other side of the hatch in the ceiling through which they supplied his food and retrieved his bucket of feces, isolated phrases like "eat this, you dog" or "have you noticed how much it smells like shit down there?" and never knowing anything, not only about his family or the world but not even when it was day and when night, when it was autumn or winter or spring again, or if they were going to kill him the following day, or the next, or if they were perhaps going to exchange him, or maybe just leave him inside, forgotten, until he gradually decomposed there alongside his feces in the airless air of that tomb and that spaceless space, with no other conversation in the end than finally shouting at his jailers, pleading, pleading with them to kill him, to please kill him already, once and for all, and not to keep him there like that any longer, and with God to take him, by all that is holy, for Him, if no one else, to take him away from there for once and for all, with nothing other than that which filled everything around him and which everything had become, the air and the space and likewise his brain, and which sometimes was time and other times was outright anguish, thick, solid, piercing anguish, diffuse, pitiless anguish that with an eye to rounding up and keeping everything for itself, made off even with the secret of whether he was still in his right mind or if they had managed to drive him out of it, with nothing but the whole of all that all the time, that man, that man who was a man before and after he was whatever he was apart from a man, had held on to life in that filthy hole for almost a year in the lives of others, hanging on to who knows what roots on who knows what cliffs or ravines.

Not even an animal, not even the worst of animals is treated like that, he thought; not even the worst vermin is deprived for that much time not only of light and space and air and freedom but even of the company of anything other than their own excrement for such infinite lengths of time, deprived even of all sight of a human face, even that of his own tormentor.

10

It was a month or two ago that Asunción, his wife, had left home; she'd gotten a job in some organization he didn't know or even care to know the nature of but that paid her a salary that was not only good, it was higher than his own, and when she came back to the apartment in one of the six identical buildings alongside the highway leading to the factory, under the pretext of stopping by to pick up something or other—take whatever you want, I've already told you, or you know what, take everything, that way I'll have more room—it seemed like her only objective was to offend him with the insinuations and reproaches she would continuously fling at him from the very moment she crossed the threshold and set foot in the house. As if there were something lacking for her if she didn't come and insult and ridicule him, he thought, as if she couldn't feel comfortable with herself or really be someone, deep down, if she didn't fight with him about something, anything, even though in fact she was the only one shouting and fighting.

"I never would've imagined that you could end up being so reactionary and fascist," she spat at him the moment she came in the last time. "So recalcitrantly reactionary and so inveterately fascist."

"I'd sure like to know what you think those words mean and what you'd know in general about any of that."

She'd had her hair cut in an odd way; it wasn't a style that gave the impression of being old-fashioned so much as what one might call primeval or primitive, sticking up in tufts, as they would have said back in the village, with very short bangs and an absurd mane that fell over the back of her neck but not down the sides, which made her face look very fat and her eyes bug out with a now strangely severe glow.

But most of the time, rather than taking the bait and answering back, he would stare at her without saying a word and remember the first years they knew one another, their dreams together, the happiness and the hardship they had shared, the good times and the not-so-good times, and how pretty and affectionate she was with him back then and had been for so long, the splendid body she had, even though she preferred to dress modestly, and how much he loved seeing her naked, because in addition to her curves, which were so impressive, it seemed he could see her entire soul. You couldn't have found a more docile, affectionate person in the whole village, he remembered her father saying to him when he went to ask for her hand, and when he saw that he had given a sort of small shudder when he heard the word *docile*, her father told him that he knew the term no longer had the same meaning among the young folk as it had before, but that it didn't mean subjugated, submissive, but rather the opposite of rigid—that she was accepting or amenable or open or something along those lines, he said.

Words lose or acquire meaning, and they may even become different words, he told himself, so why shouldn't people become different people, too. That's why he wouldn't answer her back, wouldn't enter the ring—because to whom was he going to answer back? And for what? But she, far from growing calmer when she saw he was in no mood to fight, seemed to get even more worked up by his silence, by his attitude of resignation, in which she found the excuse she needed to allow herself to give free rein to her arrogance and continue demeaning him, again and again, even though he would neither take part in the argument nor provide her, either through gesture or word or, least of all, any sort of tone that might be interpreted as rude or disrespectful, with anything she might be able to latch onto and use to keep coming at him.

"And this," she would point to a piece of furniture or a household appliance, "you'll want to keep this, too, right? Just like you guys keep everything. A traitor, you're just a traitor and a fascist, standing there like some halfwit in the town square embarrassing me in the eyes of the whole world. Your husband, they would say to me, there's your husband, you wouldn't want anything to happen to him. We don't even understand how you can be with someone like that. But you don't know anything, do you, you don't know what you owe me and Juanjo, that you owe us even the very breaths you're still able to draw, because you know so little, all you really know is how to play along with the people who exploit you and exploit our people."

Our people, our culture, our identity, and our language, us, us and them—how many times had he heard it all repeated by her and his son and so many other people? And in reference to anything at all! You might say there was nothing that couldn't eventually lead to that. At first, in light of what was evident to everyone no matter how ridiculously difficult it might at times be for them to accept it, as was often the case with self-evident things, he had a hard time not bursting out laughing; but what language, what identity, he would wonder as he listened, and he thought she'd get over it, that no one could go on being so sanctimonious with such litanies for long, and she least of all. Then, little by little, perhaps in the interest of self-preservation, he began to let it all roll off him, like water off a duck's back, as if it didn't mean anything significant, really; let them do as they like, he would say to himself, if it makes them happy, to each his own. But in the end he began to realize that more than meaning or not meaning something or having any greater or lesser foundation, those notions were above all whatever certain people wanted them to be or to mean, that they were basically weapons that they tossed around, that they wielded, that they used to feint, weapons with which they would later shoot to kill. That's when he began to hang his head and try to slip away every time she or his son spoke them or he heard anyone else saying them.

The people, in particular, was an expression that never stopped coming out of her mouth, the people this, the people that. And exploitation, too, and oppression, process, the process of liberation, and awareness-raising, and decision-making, and suffering, as well, suffering inflicted on the people and on the people's political prisoners and even on their language.

"I think it's actually you who has no idea what you're talking about, you're the one who's got her head completely mixed up, like all those people, but have it your way." That was all he could bring himself to say to her. But most of the time he didn't reply at all, he just let her talk, let her shout, let her get it all out, stood by as she let loose with broadsides of insulting and offensive remarks and began spouting off speeches in terms whose real meaning he doubted very much she'd ever stopped to think about. Patient, calm, like when you're waiting for a storm to pass and there's nothing else you can do, he would remain there, waiting, with an odd, somehow liberating restraint, impenetrable at times, his head usually bowed, his mouth shut, his melancholy-filled eyes, nevertheless, completely open.

But suddenly that last day, as if he had instantaneously reached the limits of his restraint and, without warning, the ample cup of his patience had overflowed its rim, he got up abruptly, so abruptly that he knocked the chair in which he had been enduring the habitual torrent of insults over onto the dining room floor, and he made a beeline for the sideboard. He yanked open a drawer—Asunción stood there stark still, frozen in astonishment—and without saying a word, he began rifling through it until he came across the tape measure and the chalk from his wife's old sewing box. Then he began to move the table and chairs to either side of the dining room, dragging them with uncharacteristic rage and ferocity, not caring that he was making enough noise to wake the devil, and availing himself of the newspaper from the day of the industrialist's release, without stopping for breath, he set to sketching out on the floor in one corner of the room, with mathematical precision, the edges that formed an outline analogous to the hole in which the man, pleading with his jailers to kill him already, had spent almost a year of his existence buried underground.

Half squatting, half kneeling on the floor tiles—the table and chairs were piled up in a jumble next to the television—he drew a rectangle in the corner of the dining room, thirteen feet, nine and one-third inches long by two feet, five and one-half inches wide, and once drawn, once the shape was completed and not a single inch was missing, he went over it again, diligently, painstakingly, until the chalk was completely spent in his hands, all the while repeating, over and over again, like a record with a skip, thirteen feet, nine and one-third inches long by two feet, five and one-half inches wide.

When he'd finished (two of the sides of the rectangle were formed by the right-angled walls of the dining room, and the others by just the chalk lines), he got up, regarded it for a few seconds that could have been an eternity—you might say that he put the space into his eyes—and he told her to get inside. He said it the first time with a strange calmness, get inside, would you, please, he said to her, come on, get inside, but since Asun only stared and stared at him as if he had suddenly lost his mind, he said it again, in almost exactly the same tone of voice—get inside, Asunción, would you, please, get inside—after which, since she still remained impassive, unable to believe what she was seeing or hearing, he shouted it suddenly in such a sharp tone of voice, so aggressively and unexpectedly violently, that there was nothing for her to do but to do what he said and step at once into the chalk rectangle.

"OK," he went on, having regained his calm, "OK. Now, imagine that where there is a chalk line, instead of the chalk line there is a wall, a solid wall, windowless and damp up to the ceiling, and it closes everything off and you can't see or hear a thing beyond it. Imagine you're not here, but there, inside, shut up between those walls, and you don't know where you are or what you're under or how deep you are, and now imagine time passing there. Start breathing, that's right, now start breathing with more difficulty and imagine that you're in there one day, then another day, and then another day, until a week that you can't even tell is a week goes by with you in there, shitting and pissing into a pot that someone will collect from you when they bring you your rations, and you in turn stretch to reach up and give them your pot of feces with the same hand you then use to grab your rations, and it's like that one day, and the next day, and a week, and then another week, and you try at first to take those four steps; go ahead, do it! I told you to do it! Do you hear me? Take those four goddamn steps! That's it, again, and again, ten, a hundred, a thousand, two thousand, a million times so you don't go crazy, so you don't spend the infinity of every moment stretched out on your cot looking up at a bulb that's always lit right over your face or hearing nothing but the hammering of desperation in your brain, the dripping of time in your brain, and the banging in your brain or maybe of your own head against the wall and the weakened tangle of your body falling onto the cot again and again, one day, and another, and another, for more than three hundred days. Did you hear what I just said?" he shouted. "Did you hear what I just said? Or maybe you don't have ears or eyes or a heart anymore, just an idiotic anger rotting you from within?"

He realized that he was glaring at her with a degree of vehemence and fury he didn't believe he'd ever looked at anyone with before, and then he left abruptly—he opened the door, went slowly down the stairs, and set off to walk. That night, as if it were the most natural thing for him to do, as if more than an inclination or a necessity, it were his true character, the activity and the place in which everything that could be conceived of in terms of people and things, and everything impenetrable that in the end existed within everything became plain, he once again walked along what was most likely the only place he knew how to walk along anymore, on the shoulder of the road by the metalworks and the tire retread shop and the long hangar with the high, windowless wall against which he felt particularly helpless as he passed, and afterward by the gas station with its lot full of trucks, which gave him the impression they would run him over as he crossed it, even though they were parked, and then finally the warehouse and the automobile dealership and the interchange, and that brought him to the factory.

When he got to the gate—the halberd tips on the top of the fence would become oddly stamped in his memory—he stopped for a moment and then went on again, mile after mile, to the next town. Once there, in the only bar open at that time, now well into the wee hours, he ordered something to eat and consumed it slowly at the counter, unhurriedly, with his gaze fixed not really on any one thing or another but, you might say, on the gaze itself. You might come to the conclusion that he wanted to intentionally engender suspicion, or maybe just the opposite, that he was endeavoring, poorly as it were, to go unnoticed, but after a while he called the waiter over, paid him with the same unhurriedness, and the same expression, and the same indecipherable attempts to either create mistrust or to hide it that he had exhibited while seated there on that barstool eating, and he started walking again in the opposite direction, toward the factory.

Cars zoomed by, whipping up the air beside him, and some of them honked at him or sped close past him, but not even to the trucks that seemed as if they were going to tip him over, swallowing him up in the great pockets of emptiness they created in their wake, did he seem to pay attention. The vehicles' headlights coming toward him illuminated him intermittently, dazzling him, and even though he usually stayed as far onto the shoulder as he could—a man on the side of the road, he recalled, a man on the shoulder of the road, that's what you are, or what you've become—in those wee hours everything seemed to indicate that he had forgotten the meaning of distances and margins.

When he arrived back at the factory fence topped with heavy iron bars in the shape of halberds, he sat down next to one of the pillars at the closed gate and slowly fell asleep, scrunched in an increasingly tighter ball.

Dawn had not quite completely broken when the kidnapped industrialist, who had that very day come back to work, early, woke him up. What a coincidence,

he said, surprised to have found him there in such a
state, as he helped him up, but one of the first things I
wanted to do was to thank you and everyone else for
what you've done.

"There's no need to thank us," he responded, getting
up with some difficulty. His body had gone completely
stiff and his eyes were bleary; it seemed it was going to
take a while for him to warm up.

"It's not going to be an easy thing for you all to
go on living here now," the industrialist continued, not
finding the conversation as easy to sustain as he would
have liked.

"It's never an easy thing to go on living, if you come
right down to it."

11

A little more than a year after that morning, the factory
was acquired by a multinational group that wasted
no time enacting a large-scale workforce reduction
plan. The company had begun to fare badly; the
kidnapped industrialist, who must have been the one
who really held the reins and to whom fell the heavy
task of making the most important strategic decisions,
had not succeeded in overcoming the depression he'd
fallen into after his kidnapping, and his dedication
to his work had suffered greatly, so the company, not
being able to rely on him as before, had, apparently at
the very first sign of trouble, begun slowly but surely
to drift, and according to what people were saying,

that was the reason it had ended up being not only sold off, but sold at a loss. Among other provisions, the personnel adjustment immediately established by the new ownership would include a series of early retirement offers, and Felipe Díaz Carrión, not thinking twice, accepted one without batting an eye. Truth is, it was like an act of God, his son Felipe said. An act of God, he repeated. An act of God.

He would go back to the village, to his house with the great door and the bronze knocker and the patio with the old cherry tree that his father, may he rest in peace, had planted, and back, too, to his field and his road by the river. At least there he wouldn't have to put up with anyone threatening him or giving him the evil eye just for going about his business, threatening you and who knows what all else, certain friends would say to him. With the money from the retirement payout, he could fix up the house, as far as possible, and still underwrite part of the costs his younger son's university education required, at least at first. He wanted to study biology and go live in Madrid; he had already agreed with a couple acquaintances of his who were also leaving the area, as a lot of people were, and were going to open a restaurant in Madrid that they would hire him on as a waiter for as long as things were going well. We'd have to be doing really badly not to be able to hire him at least for the weekends, they assured him.

Asunción kept the apartment, which they had finally finished paying off just a short while earlier, in one of the six identical buildings alongside the highway leading to the factory; she also kept the furniture that was so garish it seemed to be arguing with whoever was using it and whatever other objects it was meant to be used with. And he held on to the field by the river and the house on the outskirts of the village, which had belonged to his father, and before that to his grandfather, and which his great grandfather had, according to what he had heard from them, apparently built when he came back from America with just enough money for a place to live, which wasn't much compared to the elegant magnificence of the typical homes of Spaniards returning from America.

"I'm going back to the country," he'd said to Asunción over the phone.

"You've always loved that precious countryside of yours," she replied sarcastically.

"That must be it."

Asunción had been elected as a councilwoman in the most recent municipal elections, representing a party everyone knew all there was to know about without actually having to know anything. People wondered whether her son Juanjo, whom nobody called Juanjo anymore, but Potote, and who'd been working in France and whom he hadn't seen in more than two years, might not have been involved in some way in her election. One day, one day during the final month he spent working at the chemical factory, he'd gone to eat his sandwich with his coworkers at a bar nearby—it was his birthday, sixty years old, sixty big ones, so it was up to him to treat everyone— and he found himself mesmerized by a photograph in the newspaper he had used, following his general practice, to wrap up his sandwich before leaving the house. Next to three other women, sporting that exact same hairstyle that was not so much old-fashioned as it was primeval or primitive, Asunción posed for the camera with a smile he attempted to recognize and that ended up seemingly gnawing at him from within. The photograph was taken in the same square where he, alongside a few others, had gone, every day at the exact same time, week after week for almost a year, to call for the release of a man buried alive; you might even say, if you looked closely, as he was doing, that it was the exact same spot where they themselves had stood behind their banner, swallowing the ire and malevolence of certain people and the indifference or cowardice of others, in order not only to demand, by their mere presence, respect for a single person's life and freedom but to remind everyone of what, in a supposedly civilized country, you would think it might not be necessary to remind anyone of anymore, and yet it was necessary to do so, over and over again, unflaggingly, and that was, namely, that every person sees and thinks in his own way but that, as convinced as someone may feel that he is right about something, or in the right about something— you can always convince yourself of whatever you like and for whatever reason, his father always used to say—that doesn't mean that other people are under any obligation to see and think like him, nor that that person has the right to any such thing, much less any right that could be assigned pretty words and turned into some sort of standard or smokescreen, and that a person can even do whatever he wants, as he liked to explain again and again, but not just whatever he feels like.

"You just don't get it, Felipe," they said to him again as they watched him stare unblinkingly at the photo of his wife on the page of a newspaper he now bought himself. "You know it, but you don't want to admit it."

He had unwrapped his sandwich, slowly smoothed out the paper, moving the palm of his hand across the photo, which he didn't take his eyes off even for a moment, and it was as if that simple act of passing his hand back and forth over the wrinkled surface of the newspaper were the only thing that could allow him to stand looking at it, by presenting it to him intermittently, in brief flashes, just like the headlights of the cars and trucks passing him as he walked at night along the shoulder of the highway.

So that's it, he said to himself upon arriving home that day a bit after nightfall, that's it. In her smile in the photograph, which he hadn't managed to decipher at first, a strangely veiled smile, a smile someone who had known her a long time might call an artificial smile, *small-town*, that was the term that sprang to mind, though he didn't know why, a small-town smile, you could see the impassable distance that separated them and had been growing at the same pace and to the same proportions as that smile that had been forming on her face. It wasn't her smile, that was the first thing that occurred to him, or rather it wasn't the smile of the person he had first met, instead it seemed more like his son's smile the last time they could be said to have spoken to one another, when he'd actually said *my son, do you understand, my son?* Her smile also revealed, more than anything else, more than thankfulness or satisfaction at having gotten the post, and much more, especially, than any real happiness or joy, which were completely absent, something else—rivalry, hostility, and in the end repulsion, a grimace of concentrated, defiant repulsion and an air of self-satisfied, vindictive stubbornness identical to his son's expression the last time he'd called him *my son* and spoken to him as one speaks to a son. *Juanjo*, he sounded out each syllable as he walked along the shoulder of the highway, past the immense, windowless hangar next to which he could never figure out why he felt so vulnerable and alienated. *Juan José, my son, Juan José.*

If the syllables of a person's name could contain some meaning and weren't just expanding pockets or metallic hollowness, that nocturnal utterance of his would surely encompass it all. Are emotions, he put it to himself, what give meaning to names? Or love, even when thwarted or unrequited? Or is it just desperation?

The cars blinded him for a moment as they passed; it was drizzling again, and in the brief interval of time in which their headlights lit up the road in front of him, he could see the water falling almost half-heartedly. Although it was gradually soaking him, he liked to see the raindrops for the instant they hung there; they filled with light, and the dark background against which they shone seemed, just then, less dark, less able to attract and absorb everything, to swallow it all up. He went on watching them as he walked—

when he came to a puddle on the shoulder, he would quicken his pace, so that any cars driving close to the curb wouldn't splash him—and then suddenly he had the urge to see the laughing eyes and warm, calm expression of the woman he had fallen in love with almost forty years ago. He remembered what both of them always said had been the happiest day of their lives together, the day they were dead set on insisting, despite the dates not adding up right, that they'd conceived their first child.

It was a dry, Sunday afternoon, and the heat felt as if it couldn't be any more oppressive, and the sky, so clear you could almost reach out and touch it, as if it were something solid, nevertheless made you feel as though it were softly embracing everything in its care. Under the poplars, in the field, lying on the grass in the shelter of elders and danewort, everything was good, so good they could never remember it having ever been as good before or since. The leaves on the trees, swaying in the intermittent breeze, created a play of tremors of light and flashes of shadow on the pristine nakedness of her body, like sequins on the exigent mystery of her pubis and the manifest fullness of her breasts. For a moment he thought—or perhaps it was now that he was thinking it—that it was uncertain whether the light was coming from on high, from the clear flesh of the sky, or from below, from the smooth sun of her body. Above and below, just like matter and spirit, din and silence, were dimensions no longer counterposed; they became superposed, like their bodies and the fluids and the breath emanating from their bodies. In a place of no sound, you could hear the whispering of the foliage, the twittering of birds, the disquieting exactitude of water flowing in the river right nearby, and the deep breathing—her soft moaning—each time he, with a tranquility that seem to emerge from the very earth on which they were lying, penetrated her as if he had done no other thing in life, nor believed he ever would, than enter her.

He was aware at the time, or rather now, that there were doubtless many ways to say what he was doing and many words with which to say it—I'm fucking her, for example, or I'm laying her, I'm boning her, giving it to her, or I'm screwing her brains out, he could have put it, or perhaps he expressed it the way his friends always expressed it—but it seemed to him that none of those even came close to what was happening there and that, just the opposite, they were creating an unfillable space between what was going on there and how to express it, between what they were doing, or, rather, what was happening, and what was done or what happened by naming it, a gulf that, for all the words or ways of expressing it he might try, continued growing wider rather than narrower.

You can't know, he said to himself, you can't know what is really being said when you say it. He understood gratitude and tenderness when he picked a piece of fruit or observed the slowness of growth in a plant or the blossoming of a bud; he understood skill when he grafted one branch onto another or composed a sentence at the printshop, when he released a spring, when he wielded a tool; he knew about violence from digging and about vigor from grabbing a lump of earth and breaking it into pieces, and he knew, too, about exhaustion and satisfaction, but all that—tenderness and violence, vigor and fatigue, skill and satisfaction—was just one part of that which was nevertheless much more than all of it put together. A body that calls out to another body, a body that is no longer a body, however, because of its being so much something else, and tenderness that is no longer tenderness, because of its being so much body and flesh, secreted fluids and oozing pores, licking tongues and sucking lips and also blood and nerves and mud with no need for anything to resort to words that might come later, just like the Egyptian vultures or the great, bearded vultures adhering to their agreement.

He fell asleep with his hand in the mud of the irrigation ditch that ran at the foot of the elders, and embracing her again after he awoke, he accidentally smeared her side and cheek with muck. She laughed—or perhaps the foliage, the river, and the birdsong laughed—with a calm, gentle peal that gave him the feeling he could see through the world for just an instant, and the world was good and cheerful and it reached everything and everywhere. Without knowing what moved him to it, motivated, perhaps, by the incitement of this unveiling, he went on slowly slathering her entire body with mud, and when he had finished, he stretched out on the ground to rest, thinking that everything was finished and, therefore, everything could now begin.

Perhaps obeying the same instinct, she, too, went to gather mud from the irrigation ditch and then set about rubbing it over his face, over his forehead and his cheeks and his mouth, to the point of pretending to suffocate him, and then over his chest and his legs and his pubic area. Completely coated, as if they were mud sculptures of themselves, they began gamboling and gesturing and moving like primitive creatures, fragile creatures, but at the same time creatures of great power who shrieked without words and moved without meaning, and then, giving themselves no time to laugh or howl, they sprang toward the riverbank and, sunken deeply into the silt, he dissolved his mud into hers and into the river's mire, penetrating her again as if that would allow him to encompass everything, just as the mud had soaked in through their pores and mucked up their hair and their bodies and thus become one with them somehow forever. Then they rested, a rest to end all rests, the resting of matter in matter, of breath in light, the resting of image in mud, of cessation in the river, of creation in nothingness.

After a time, after a time they'd have been hard pressed to judge whether infinite or infinitesimal, a single instant, and as if there existed something to be frightened of in the face of such unaltering plenitude, they leapt up and ran to a pool in the river a few yards away. Until that moment, until that moment that seemed to him to contain or to be the consummation of all the previous moments of his life, he had always swum there alone, or in the company of his father, but from that day on, the memory of the smell of her body that afternoon, of her body or the mud, and the memory of the shrieking and the laughter, the dunking and the flailing and the splashing of that time so infinite and yet so fleeting, would conjure up for him, indelibly and forever, the sound and the smell of paradise, the raindrops, lit up and hanging there for just a moment, that would make the dark background against which they shone have less power to absorb everything and swallow it all up.

Suddenly, shots rang out from some poacher, disorienting them. They couldn't tell if they had sounded from far away or close by, just behind them, or if they'd just begun or it had been going on for a good while and they'd only noticed them right then, and they hurried back to look for their clothes, as if they'd only just then realized they were naked. She wanted to cover herself with her hands as soon as she got out of the water, her breasts and her pubic area and her face if she could have, and he thought about doing it, too, but then he burst out laughing. What are you doing, he asked her. Don't tell me you're embarrassed?

PART TWO

12

Back in his village, to which he had been returning for a few days at a time in summers, at first with his wife and two sons and then gradually only occasionally, with Felipe, a good part of the people he had known and who had made up his world had either died or gotten very old, some sick and in wheelchairs in the nursing home, others debilitated, feeble, and weak, and those he remembered as energetic and chatty were now often listless or just waiting out their time.

It's true that some houses had been fixed up or, as people put it, made decent, but it had been done with a new, out-of-control sort of bad taste that was contagious—contagious as only stupidity can be, he recalled having heard his father say—and stood out even more in a place where what little there was was at least harmonious and could therefore seem like a lot. Neither the materials used—he thought—nor the improvement ideas they had come up with were appropriate there, and they would never be appropriate, and that's just the cases when the old houses, some of which were unquestionably valuable and elegant, hadn't been torn down completely in order to erect bland apartment buildings like the one he'd been living in for the past twenty years.

You might say that from a certain moment on, people had stopped caring a fig—a flying fig, he emphasized, not a whit, less than a whit—about what had been in those places before or how things were done before; people had begun not to care even the least bit about things that were right in front of their noses, or beside them, or behind them. Their relationship with the adjacent, he said to himself, their relationship with the adjacent, and he stopped then to think a moment. Everything seemed to have begun continually bumping up against everything else, lines, dimensions, shapes, all bumping up against everything, against everything except bad taste and conceit. Could this be the new thing, the new era? And what comes after bad taste, he wondered. What came before conceit?

Even the insides of houses had changed, and when he visited people at their homes, the same accumulation of junk, furniture, and the most disparate of décor, which seemed to be arguing with its own owners, was at times suffocating to him, even from the very first moment of stepping inside. How eager everyone is to fling themselves into the arms of the worst, to thoughtlessly abandon whatever little or much they actually have!—he marveled. Is it really so hard to figure out how to embrace the best of the new and set aside the worst of the old that people so often end up doing just the opposite? What pride in one's own judgment and what stubbornness of vision doesn't run the risk of eventually taking hold of everything?

"I'm going to leave everything as is," he said to his son Felipe. "I'll install heating, I'll change the plumbing and the lighting fixtures, the bathroom and a few things in the kitchen, and the rest will stay the same. White, with the same sideboard and the same pantry and the same four chairs as always, which I'll have reupholstered. How does that seem to you?"

It seemed good to him, and it also seemed to him that his father now had the chance to remake his life, to resume it, to breathe again the breath of things that had made him what he was and afforded him the fortitude he possessed, and foremost among the first several things he resumed, just as if it were actually himself he was resuming, was his walk along the road to the field by the river.

But that day, which might rightly be said to be the first day in twenty years when he went back to doing what he should probably never have stopped doing in the first place, when he saw that the weather had quickly turned as stormy as it had been on the last of the afternoons he had walked along the road after having walked along it almost daily for so many years, he wondered what that coincidence might mean, if things in fact meant anything, or if they merely happened and we were the ones who implored them to say something to us.

Do things resume when we resume them?—he put the question to himself again. Or is it simply that we give free rein to a feeling of nostalgia for something that has gone forever because it is in its nature to be always going, not only in terms of time but even of space, away from us, and perhaps in exactly the same measure as we ourselves are going?

13

Just as on that other day twenty years ago that was so different and yet such a mirror image of this one, as soon as he sensed the storm descending on him, he gathered everything up hurriedly and locked the old door that time and lack of care had turned completely gray. Without pausing even a moment, so that the downpour wouldn't catch him out on the road, he went up the pathway flanked by patches of elder, bisnaga, and danewort until he got to the path that would take him back to the village. In total, from the little door of gray, rotten wood to the great, sturdy door with the bronze knocker at his house on the outskirts of the village, it wasn't much more than two and a half miles along a road that was much more than a mere road to him or a simple connection between two points, it was in fact his character and the mettle of his life, the nature of his inclination toward the world, and his renunciation of or disappearance from it. It was also a good portion of his understanding, as if he had gradually been forging his experience of life and his relationships with people on that path, on that low coming and going and ruminating on what he saw and seeing what he was ruminating about, on that measured placing and settling of things, seeing the common in the different and seeing things that were the same differently, accepting the slings and sorrows of life—by allowing the positive to reign—gradually moving beyond his personal emptinesses and solitudes while listening to the impenetrable sound of the water in the river and the wind in the leaves of the poplar trees, which he interpreted differently depending on the day and the light and the season. That, perhaps more than any other source, is where he got that sort of silent energy of his from, and his rare, taciturn, melancholic wisdom, which was as thoughtful as could be imagined and at the same time resolute and forceful, and which some people chalked up, for the sake of chalking it up to something, to his reading.

Well-read? Me?—he would usually object. That is to say, reading, as in reading, I mean, I've read a little (and if he was at his house, he would point out the two or three stacks of books he had obviously read and reread in detail), but really what I've done is to listen, to listen to my father, may he rest in peace, what little I could and to listen to whomever might be speaking to me, to listen and above all to see, he would stress, to look around with my eyes as open as I could make them or as open as others would let me.

At the beginning, before reaching the immense hulk of Pedralén from the field by the river, the road curved two times along the hills to the right, while on the other side, by the river's edge, there grew in rows a thick, broad stand of black poplars, whose leaves would whisper when the wind blew through them and always kept him company with their questions and which spread their coolness and their memories along the length of the path. The leaves sounded odd that day, as if they were nervous or anticipating something, and he went around the grove more quickly and less calmly than he could recall ever having done before. But despite his hurry, despite the fact that it wouldn't have been in the least an exaggeration to say that the storm was now upon him, when he arrived at the imposing wall of stone, he could not but slow his pace, as he'd done when he'd passed by earlier in the other direction, and pause to lay his eyes a moment on the modest, stone cross that had been erected there, directly below the highest point of the rock, one of the years he'd been absent from the village.

It was at the beginning of the autumn of '77, during the days when changes in the entire country seemed to finally accelerate, when the town council decided to erect that somberly sculpted cross that measured a bit more than a yard off the ground. It had been hewn from the same stone as the immense crag that rose on the other side of the road, and the footing that served as its base, also from the same stone, had several names chiseled into it. Some of them, three, had full first and last names, while two others had only one last name. Among these latter was his father's name, Felipe Díaz, Felipe Díaz Díaz, in fact, but since it was only the name and the first surname, it could easily have been his father's or his second son's or even his own. He would have liked to smile this time, too, but all at once, as if something inside him had suddenly turned on a hinge forged from the murky metal of an enigma, he became enshrouded in a strangely indecipherable expression.

After the rocky ravine of Pedralén, where the Egyptian vulture kept its nest from mid-February well into August, there was still more than three-quarters of the road left before he got to his house on the outskirts of the village. On the other side of the river, completely unaware of the approaching storm, the watchers who were following the progress of the vultures from the wide shoulders of the highway seemed to continue impassively with their pastime. What's more, it seemed that the imminence of the storm, far from upsetting them, seemed to actually increase the attraction for them, and so you could see them watching ecstatically—probably for the last time that year, since there could only be a short time left until they emigrated to other climes—as the vultures soared and glided, their wings extended as if they wanted to embrace all that immensity. They gazed unconcernedly and coolly toward the break in the ridge, they watched the nests, they watched the imposing, intimidating flights of the vultures or waited calmly for them to return from their long absences in search of carrion; although it's possible—and there was no evidence to the contrary—that some of them were focusing on him, on his tiny, defenseless progress past the foot of the immense rock, beneath the circling flight, perhaps, of an Egyptian vulture.

Egyptian vultures—he always remembered how his father had told him at this same spot, impressing him

to the point of awe, when he was still very small—
were the first to arrive where there was carrion, at
times even to the point that one might think they
had gotten to the victim while it was still in its death
throes or that they had somehow prepared the ground
and even created the opportunity. But the fineness
of their beaks, their slightness, or, if you like, their
delicacy, only allowed them to slurp down the soft
part of the carcasses; the soft parts, his father would
repeat, oddly pensive, thinking, most likely, about other
things, the soft parts, like eyes and tongues. That's why
they need the larger vultures, the black vulture and the
griffon vulture and the bearded vulture—he would
explain—to rip apart the carcasses beforehand, so that
they could then enjoy the victims' soft remains. It's
the preeminence of savages, he would conclude, the
privilege of the shrewd. The high-handed agreement
among scavengers, Felipe Díaz Carrión would think
later, the tacit, instinctive, and at the same time highly
rational agreement of the great, black vultures of
terrifying wingspan, greater even than that of eagles,
and the elegant, white, Egyptian vulture that devours
victims' entrails and leaves them with no eyes, and no
tongue.

He also remembered his father telling him on several
occasions that even though it wasn't at all inconceivable
for a person to mistake an Egyptian vulture at first
glance for a stork, a scavenger that devours carcasses for
the avian symbol of fertility and good omens, you need
only look beyond the similar coloring of the plumage
and focus closely, even if only for a moment, on the

neck and the feet to see right away that the Egyptian vulture's were much shorter and less slender than the stork's. Of course, you had to look closely.

It was like everything in life, he told him, some things are and some things aren't, but those things, the one's that aren't, sometimes end up doing much more than the things that are. The mysteries of life, he concluded—and at this point it always seemed to him that he could hear the whispering of the wind in the leaves of the poplar trees or the babbling of the water in the river—the mysteries of life and the state of things.

That's why you always have to try to identify everything in the exact place and form you come across it, he would often insist, and to identify things without prejudging them, without absolutes and without thoughtlessness and without rhetoric, and without shrinking from this responsibility, because confusion—or an inflexible position—doesn't generally lead to anything good or clear, and the people who always benefit from it are generally the least desirable.

He didn't understand, he would listen to the murmuring of the air in the leaves and the shrubs along the road when his father spoke to him, but he didn't understand it, despite the fact that he got the vague feeling, although he didn't know why, that buried within this non-understanding of his was a particular form of comprehension that now, many years later, he could plainly see had been bearing fruit. It all depends on how you walk over and over again along that road, he thought.

14

With the crag of Pedralén now behind him, the road
back grew progressively but imperceptibly wider and
ceased to be a mere bridle trail. On the left-hand
side, on the return route, the low, mortarless stone
walls, often crowned with brambles, marked the
boundaries of the different plots, or sometimes it was
a line of black poplars or elms, once more struggling
to overcome Dutch elm disease. Beyond these
walls—a few pomegranate trees, heavy with fruit this
year, poked up from behind one of them—the fields
stretched as far as the river; meanwhile, on the right,
as if the overwhelming fertility of the other side of the
road had wanted to display there its exact opposite, just
the way things often do, changing from one minute
to the next into their adverse, isolated sections of dry
hills populated by gorse and thyme jutted up, the path
the only break between them. The road skirted slowly
around those slopes, around the hillsides and mud-filled
gullies, until it came to the old abandoned mill, where
the packed-earth that had been gradually widening
then became an asphalt roadway no longer fit only for
pack animals and men walking on foot—and probably,
although it would be hard to say why, in silence—and
led over and old, stone bridge and into the sprawling
outskirts of the village.

As he reached the first streets—the sky had been
impeccably blue but had given way again, just like that

afternoon twenty years ago, and you might say almost just as suddenly, to a cottony landscape of ever more threatening clouds—a hurricane-force wind suddenly began sweeping everything up and sending everything haywire, as if it could no longer bear to have things where they were. Little whirlwinds of dust and dirt were kicked up everywhere and every which way; tumbleweeds and gritty particulates like multiple BB blasts stuck like tiny needles in his cheeks and forehead, and the dust, the dust everywhere, as if everything had been turned into to dust, it got into the corners of your eyes as if to ensure that nothing at all, least of all your sight, could remain safeguarded from that vortex.

How difficult it is to always imagine, before something throws everything into a frenzy, all the many things that could fall at any moment, that could suddenly totter and break into pieces or become instantly shut down forever, all the things that could possibly go wrong. Only the plastic bags, inflated and puffy, had a hard time falling; they were full of the very thing that was sending everything else out of control, and so they remained airborne for a long time, tossed capriciously back and forth.

Then suddenly—just like the other time, there was no one left out on the streets, rushing cars, closing doors—the first isolated drops began to fall, giant, fat drops, of a girth so incomprehensibly fat that they pounded into the dust that had piled up on the sides of the roads with a muted sound, damped out, as if they were smothering something spread out and thin. For a moment it seemed that everything was suspended, the water, the dust, the blades of grass, and the plastic bags in the air, and that everything was anticipation or fear, imminence and lying in wait, but in a flash—as if the sky had ripped open, as the phrase on many people's lips in such cases goes—a torrential rain accompanied by colossal thunderclaps that echoed with strange, evocative power suddenly began to shake everything, to soak everything and overflow everything and spill out everywhere. The storm drains couldn't keep up, and in no time at all there formed great torrents of water that swept everything in their paths—sticks, grass, plastic scraps, and cans—along newly-formed streams that rounded up water from drain pipes and sloshing gutters as if hoping to encompass it all, engulf it all, and inundate it all. The worst thing, Felipe, Felipe Díaz Carrión, had repeated many times over the course of those twenty years, perhaps recalling these end-of-summer storms, might not be so much what's happening now, no matter how dreadful that may be, but that the particulates and dust that get in your eyes blind you and prevent you from seeing it beforehand, and then anything can happen, anything.

15

At the beginning of October, the first October he spent back in the village, his son Felipe announced he was paying him a surprise visit. I'll get there at around dinnertime, he'd said, before hanging up the phone in what seemed to him a brusquer manner than usual. Plus, it was Saturday, and like all Saturdays and holidays, assuming he hadn't been fired from the restaurant or something else had happened, he thought, he was supposed to be working. That weekend job of his allowed him to underwrite part of his room, board, and tuition in Madrid, and he was very proud of it, so this visit, as happy as it made him, couldn't but seem odd to him. Something's going on, he conjectured. But beyond this first moment of suspicion, which had been affixing itself to his character like lichen to the bark of a tree, the joy of seeing his son again quickly prevailed; he must want a weekend away to relax, he thought, what's so strange about that, or maybe he even wants to go foraging for mushrooms to bring back to the restaurant.

He hadn't seen him at all since the end of August, when he'd come to stay with him for a couple of weeks and spent the mornings helping him in the fields. He only called him from time to time to see how he was doing and tell him about some adventure or other of his in Madrid and, more than anything, to reminisce about their early-morning, summer walks along the road by the river. Much of the time they walked in silence, and other times, as their usual custom had always been, commenting on the plants they were seeing or on the progress and state of the crops in the fields—if you go down there, you'll see the henbane, his father told him the first day—but whether they were silent or talking, listening to the rhythmic sound of their footsteps on the dirt or the quiet voices of their inner thoughts and conversations, the two of them seemed to move along with a serenity that one might call a prolongation or emanation of the road itself, because perhaps it's possible that just as a pebble can get into your shoe, there is something that can also get inside you and make your blood flow at that same, ideal pace at which water rushes along a river or leaves adapt effortlessly to the wind. Roads remove self-conceit, his father had told him one morning, they draw importance away from things that don't have it in order to give it, but in a more resignedly sensible way, to that which does truly possess it.

But when they got to the small, stone cross beneath the promontory of Pedralén, they always stopped for a while; they would go over and over their memories and they would go over the names as if they needed to remember them all again and read them all again, and when they got to Felipe Díaz, both of them, every time, would think how this could be the name of either one of them, or how, in fact, it already was. They would be quiet then, though it wasn't a silence of no words, it was more a din of words crowding together, colliding into each other, and piling onto one another until they were effectively neutralized and remained in the end always on the impotent, stunned brink of the impenetrable, of that which is essentially and necessarily ungraspable despite being the simplest thing in the world and always being the same, like that road, or as if the inexhaustible power of those questions we are least able to respond to, despite not doing anything else in this life other than trying to respond to them, were eternally springing from that which is always the same and the simplest.

The pandemonium of the simple, he recalled having heard his father say and having thought, himself, on several occasions, the thundering of the silent, the violent discord of that which is self-evident—namely, that one is born, and one dies, like leaves and plants; that the days pass quickly, like water in the river, and that in them there are good hours and also hours that are decidedly bad, or worse (as happens with people, too, for that matter, there are bad ones and then those who are worse still, his father—Grandfather—would always say, and you never knew if he said it jokingly, or half-jokingly, or perhaps in utter seriousness); and that sometimes things turn out well and you come out ahead and then other times you lose or things come out badly, or even really, really badly, but that's what character is for, mettle, his grandfather would say, and his father would say, mettle with which to face it all head-on, the same way the road faced the slopes and the arid gullies of the hills, and even the sheer face of Pedralén, and also the sweet span of overwhelmingly fertile land next to the river, never with any histrionics or fuss, never with any anxiety or excessive yearning (renunciation, instead), but always in the most workable, clean, well-adjusted, and practicable way, and most of the time as if it were the easiest thing in the world.

Rare was the day, once the stone cross was left behind and they were walking past the poplar grove on the final, remaining stretch before getting to the field, that they didn't end up talking about Grandfather.

"But he must have done something besides, there must have been some reason?" his son never tired of inquiring in one way or another.

Despite the many times he'd told him about the whole thing, it seemed he was never satisfied, that something was always missing, some bit of information or some detail that, despite its being miniscule or trivial on the surface, would never at its base be too insignificant for him to latch onto and use to explain to himself, in no matter how conceited or circuitous a way, that which he had always considered to be unjustifiable. To be able to go on trusting that men are not the evil beasts his grandfather, may he rest in peace, seemed to have always believed deep down that many of them were when given the slightest opportunity.

"It's a lot to take in, I know; who would know better than I?" his father would always respond with more or less the same words each time. "But that's the way it is, simple as that. Slice it however you like, there isn't any more to it than that, no matter how you add it up."

As for the rest, he concluded one day, though I may be getting out of my depth and into the kind of deep water where one always falls short or gets in over his head, that's how it must have always been and that's how it is still, and you've got to add to the tremendous pain of events, as if that alone weren't enough, the pain that causes incredulity in others, incredulity and indifference. You tell them something and they don't believe you. They think, or it's convenient for them to think, that there has to be something more to it. Or maybe they don't care, they don't care a proverbial fig just so long as it doesn't affect them, and so in the end you're not able to tell anyone anything, and you don't even want to. That pain, and maybe not so much the other pain, the original pain, and listen carefully to what I'm saying here, that's the pain that does you in in the end and pushes you to the verge of desperation and the brink of who knows what. Other people don't want to know, they would prefer to act as if it had nothing whatsoever to do with them, they weasel out, and they brush you off, thinking well he must have done something or to each his own; they'll grow such a carapace of indifference and a coating of avoidance and cowardice will become so encrusted on their own skin that they'll end up becoming inseparable from them and allowing themselves to be pickled from within by the vilest of all concoctions, a mindset that mistakes the victim for the perpetrator and gives the one the sort of treatment and consideration that corresponds to the other. Of course, the best way to believe or realize something is to have it happen to you one day. As long as it doesn't happen to you, they'll say, sealing the admission of their own disregard and lack of solidarity. But sometimes, not even that is enough—he concluded—not even that.

16

That early-October day, as soon as he got word of his son's visit and was feeling more reassured after having come up with his own explanations for it, Felipe threw the old, faded jacket he usually wore to the field over his shoulders, grabbed the old satchel he left hanging behind the kitchen door, and went straight out to pick the last of the green beans, so that his son could have them for dinner. He hadn't planned on going that day—he was still working on slowly fixing up the house—but the idea of preparing him freshly harvested vegetables seemed to suddenly give him wings. The cornfields on the riverside, though they still had a few green leaves, were already almost dried out, and the leaves on the poplars had begun to take on those yellowish hues that would soon wax golden and that had brightened his days ever since he was young, the way only true beauty, that which is eternal each time you see it, can brighten things. Look, Felipe, look, what splendor, he would remember his father saying in the most unerring tone imaginable and filled, what's more, with a sense of awe he hoped to convey to his sons as well, as if that, that tone, that tone of awe, might rank as one of the most valuable items of any inheritance.

But when his son got there, it seemed to him that he looked troubled—something's going on, he conjectured again, something's going on. After hugging him hello, he barely saw more than the backside of him as he went into his room to drop his bags and then headed back out the front door again to, he said, go buy cigarettes at the bar before it closed. I'll start dinner, he replied. It'll be ready in about an hour, so don't be too long.

He realized that more than hugging him, he had in fact thrown himself awkwardly onto him, sort of heavily and yet absently, as if he were avoiding any contact with him, in spite of his having been the one to reach out to him, and avoiding his gaze and his face the whole time. After a short while—he couldn't have been gone for even five minutes—he heard him open the door again, trace his steps back to his room, and then head toward the kitchen, where he had already begun to busy himself.

Looking up without raising his head, almost out of the corner of his eye, he saw him hurry in like someone returning in exasperation to retrieve something he had forgotten, or rather to tell him something he couldn't quite resolve whether or not to tell him, and then suddenly, looking as though he couldn't possibly be more disgusted with himself than he was at that moment, he turned on his heel once again and left the same way he had come, with the same haste and the same hesitation and the same exasperation, but not without first setting, or more like tossing, a folded newspaper, like a reflection of his own impotence, down on the table.

He hadn't gotten the chance to say anything to him, he hadn't even gotten the chance to look at him, and certainly not in the eye, and that silence, that absence of words that was so telling in the end, had unquestionably amplified the muffled sound made by the sheets of newsprint falling onto the surface of the table. *Ffflt*, went the newspaper, and *ffflt* he later recalled it continuing to resonate in his head for some time, as if it were trying to tell him something.

Nevertheless, just as he had done so many other times, he took refuge in the mechanical gestures with which one generally carries out the most everyday tasks, executing them with all the care and formality he could muster. It was almost like a prescription against unease, according to his experience, to do diligently, not so much slowly as meticulously, tasks that might seem of quite little importance, to pour your whole soul into each step, as if our entire lives were bound up in each and every detail, as they very well may be. And so he pulled out two of the middle pages from the paper his son had left there, and he laid them out on the table. He usually laid down some sort of paper when he prepared vegetables, almost always a page from the newspaper or an opened out napkin, so that he could then fold the leavings up into a cone and throw them in the garbage without having to wipe down the table again, and the paper his son had left there couldn't have come in more handy.

To one side of it, then, he put the freshly picked green beans, the carrots, potatoes, and an onion, as well as a block of lamb shoulder, and on the other, a couple of empty plates he would slowly fill up. With mechanical slowness, he scraped the skins of the carrots and then cut them lengthwise; then it was time for the potatoes, which he peeled and afterward cut into pieces as well. He cut them with a snap—first he stuck in the knife, and then, instead of slicing cleanly all the way to the bottom, at the last instant he broke the potato off, which produced that characteristic snapping sound of the finest-quality tubers. *Snap, snap* he went, with a rhythm that resounded strangely, like an echo, in the quiet emptiness of the kitchen.

And then, as the water heated in the pot, and once the onion was peeled, he removed the tips of the beans one by one, splitting them in half. Sometimes, as he cut them in two, the string from the pod would stick and come off on the knife, and he continued slowly tossing all of it, the peels and the scrapings from before and now the tips and the little strings from the tender beans, onto the unfolded pages of the newspaper that would eventually go, along with all the leavings, into the trash can. The bean tips fell steadily onto the paper a few seconds apart from one another with a flat sound, as if they were the first drops of a storm, and just as those drops slowly coat the ground, these, too, steadily came to cover the lines of text on the newspaper's surface.

To him, all those sounds resonated as if something were working to amplify them or had set its mind to prolonging them. The snap of the potato, the tiny crinkling of the bean tips as they fell onto the paper—the drops of rain on the muffled dust of the road—or the flattened sound of the newspaper on the table. At one point, an especially long string from one of the beans he was cleaning stuck to the knife—we really are coming up to the end of the season, he thought—and after dropping it contemptuously onto the spread-out paper, he noticed that it had fallen in such a way as to underscore a line of text on the upper part of the open page.

Drawn by that unusual underlining—the little string had ended up positioned almost perfectly horizontally under the printing—he looked more carefully at the paper he had been planning on later throwing away with all the leavings inside, and suddenly, as soon as he read the first two words that were underlined the best, and, immediately afterward, the following ones, it seemed to him that the kitchen, that the whole world in which he was breathing, in an instant was empty of air. But it wasn't only air that was suddenly missing, it was the floor, no longer solid, his blood, no longer flowing, the very thingness of things, their proximity, it was the dimension of space itself and the severe luminosity of light. As if everything around him had suddenly disappeared, been wiped out by a hurricane that had whisked it all at a single stroke into a state of the most indifferent insignificance, he was overwhelmed by a stupor the likes of which he believed he had never felt in his entire life, and which wasn't really a stupor, nor was it mere disconcertedness or disorientation. It was a desire for that hurricane to whisk him away, as well, to yank him up and whisk him away to where all those other things had disappeared, so that he could disappear along with them.

Two last names, he saw the two last names and then four more words before the end of the paragraph, and above them, above what was doubtless the continuation of an article that began on a previous page, was a phrase in parentheses and italics that read, "Continued from page 1." He read those six words, the four words plus the two last names, again and then again and then once more, and he didn't know if it was in the hope that one of those times they might say something other than what they said, or perhaps out of an unconscious desire to wear them out, for them to become used up or faded, and for there not to be written there what neither his incredulity nor his helplessness could prevent from being written there.

Without daring at first to keep going, or daring to do anything, in fact—his heart was so clenched it seemed like it would explode—he quickly got up to look for the rest of the newspaper. He didn't know where he could have left it after he'd pulled out the two middle pages; he didn't know how to walk, he didn't even know that things had to be in one particular place or that a single space could be so full of places, and the limp heaviness of his limbs astonished him, as did the fact that his eyes were used for seeing things and were not actually the things themselves.

But it had to be around there somewhere, it couldn't have gone very far, if only, he managed to reason, because he hadn't set foot outside the kitchen since his son had brought it in and left it lying there— *ffflt*, he recalled the sound again—right there on the table, so he couldn't *not* find it, he couldn't *not* go on scrambling around for it like a man possessed, in order to read, no matter what, that first page it said the line of text had come from. Though not exactly in order to read anything, in fact, or at least not right away, or to keep reading anything yet except the single first name that had been cut off and separated from the two last names at the beginning of the continuation of the article on the middle pages he was holding, to read it all together, one first name and two last names, and say it all together, confirming what he didn't want to confirm no matter how much he already knew, and knowing what he wouldn't ever have wanted to know no matter how many times he may have been able to sense it. It could still be a mistake, it could still be a coincidence, pure chance, they were two very common last names, after all!

He found the rest of the newspaper lying on the chair that was right in front of him, and without stopping to look at anything else, without even stopping to look at the most obvious things, the headlines and the photograph, he went straight to the last two words of the lead, front-page story. He read them once, and then he read them again, and again, looking away from the paper and then coming back to stare at the exact same spot where the two words were indelibly written. Juan José, it said clearly each time, and that's where the text on the front page came to an end, the text of the article that then continued on the middle pages of the paper, beginning with those two last names, first Díaz and then García, and then, after a comma, after a comma grammarians would have called "explanatory," the sentence reading, "who perpetrated the assassination." It said "the assassination," it said it again and again, no matter how many times he reread it hoping it would eventually say something else—"who perpetrated the assassination."

It was hard to take in the fact that his son's name had come to be present in a sentence like that, to be—as he had been taught in school—the subject of a predicate like that, "who perpetrated the assassination," "who perpetrated the assassination," or, more than hard, it was terrible in fact, the very core of terribleness, the scrapings of bitterness, as his father used to say, comparing things to fruit. His son, a murderer. His son, a murderer who has killed another person who is now no longer living and can never come back to life because his son, his own son, the fruit of his loins, has taken that person's life—the thought pounded away in his brain again and again but with a sudden, ensuing sense of calmness, as if something, some scavenger, for instance, had just dived down and stripped him of his softest parts, his heart and his lungs and also his tongue and his eyes, and so he could finally finish reading with the empty sockets of his eyes, which were now incapable of shedding tears, and the empty space of his heart, which was now incapable of registering a single beat.

With the tentativeness of someone who is afraid of breaking something or afraid that the floor on which he is walking will fall away beneath him if he walks too fast, if he doesn't take one step at a time, testing out the firmness of the pavement and the soundness of the road, he continued reading that paper he had been planning to roll up into a cone in a minute and throw into the trash along with all the leavings. "The person to whom investigators also impute," he read, "two other assassinations, that of the aforementioned journalist and anti-Francoist fighter, and that of the young Guardia Civil member," and following this, the latter's two last names, the first of which was García, like his son's, preceded by a first name he'd never heard prior to the years he'd spent walking along the highway with the metalworks and the tire retread shop after that.

Obsessed by the text itself, he hadn't even looked at the photographs yet, either the one of the murdered Law professor, the illustrious jurist, the caption said, champion of freedoms and democratic rationality, or the other one, of his son, handcuffed and being escorted by two agents, sporting a two-day shadow of a beard, a short jacket he didn't recognize, two sneakers—like always, sticking out from a pair of jeans—and, most especially, smiling, haughty, with that sarcastic smile of defiant petulance that he knew came not so much from a feeling of resolve or contempt as, more than anything else, disgust, rancor, and an air of bitter repugnance that was as incomprehensible as it was grotesque.

Without being aware of what he was doing, so mechanically, so cut off from his own self that he almost had the impression it was someone else doing it, he put a fistful of salt into the water, which had been boiling in the pot now for an amount of time he was unable to judge, and he began steadily, almost, you might say, in slow-motion, putting in the beans, the carrots and potatoes, the onion, and the block of lamb shoulder. Then, with the same slowness and the same mechanical, abstracted manner, he went about throwing the leavings into the trash, almost, you might also say, not so much like someone who is throwing things out and disposing of them but instead like someone holding onto something, like someone keeping something, setting it aside. But he didn't throw them away inside the cone of paper he usually made, instead he picked them up them with his hands, he held them unhurriedly in his hands and felt deep within himself the strange pleasure of getting them dirty, grimy, he might have put it, with the peels and the scrapings, as if only through contact with something material, something dirty and disposable, terminal, could he find not consolation or support but at the very least something to be near to. Then he opened the door to the patio, walked over to the old cherry tree his father had planted, and put his arms around the trunk, letting himself drop to the ground.

With his face pressed against the trunk, pressed so close and hard against it that it would not have been easy, given the amount of light at that hour, to say where one began and the other ended, where the skin of one ended and the sheath of the other began, he slid slowly downward, scraping his cheek as though he wanted the bits of the bark that broke off when he did so, or the sap the old trunk secreted, to stick to it, and also, most likely, so that the bark, too, could become impregnated with the blood of the scratches and scrapes it produced.

And this is the state—collapsed on the ground across the roots of the cherry tree, which had begun to lose its leaves, holding on to it in a position that seemed as compressed as it could possibly be—in which his younger son found him a short time later. He picked him up—come on, Dad, get up, let's not have this get the better of you, too—and once he was on his feet, he shook the leaves and stems from his wool sweater and wiped off his face with his handkerchief. He allowed himself to be taken in hand, he was like a dead weight and at the same time seemingly as light as a feather, and his son tried to lead him by the arm to the kitchen. I'm coming, I'm coming, don't worry, he said to him, and he refused to lean on him.

In the same mechanical, empty way he had been doing everything, he turned off the stove, removed the lid, put the plates on the table, and served the food, before finally sitting down in his chair as though he were a man at least twenty years older than the one who had just a scant few minutes ago sat in the very same chair.

17

They ate in silence, deliberately rather than slowly, bringing the food to their mouths with a strange feeling of self-awareness, spacing out their mouthfuls not so much as if it took a great deal of effort to chew but as if chewing, having something between their teeth and in their mouths, were the only way they could truly feel that they were where they were. But when they each finished their last bite, as if that were the signal to end a truce, they instantly fell to speaking, clumsily, confusedly, skirting the issue at first and almost as if reluctantly trying to trick themselves and one another by beating around the bush and dodging the question at hand, until gradually they were able to clear the way and begin navigating the obstacles and come to the point. None of this is your fault, his son said to him at last, none of this is your fault.

"Some of it must be," he immediately replied. "There must be something I didn't know how to do, or I didn't know how to say, perhaps, in the way it needed to be said or at the moment it needed to be said. There must be something, Felipe, there must be something. These things don't happen for no reason, and I'm his father."

His son explained what he knew as far as he could, what he had suspected at first and then known and later confirmed again and again through details and ever more details and from more than one person. Do you remember that day I came home from school bleeding, he said to him, because I'd gotten really good and beaten up? The fascist little brother, they called me, the asshole little brother. Every day, they wrote *Felipe Díaz* on the blackboard inside a bull's-eye, and there were even some teachers who left it up there and wouldn't erase it for the entire class.

Without budging, without uttering a word or making a single peep, his father listened with the full and complete attention of someone who, more than listening, is in fact seeing what is being told. But at a certain point, at a point that must have coincided with the mention of a bull's-eye, inside a bull's-eye, he began to repeat over the top of his son's words, as if they were a counterpoint to them, the exact sentences from the newspaper he had just read, again and again. The perpetrator, the perpetrator of the assassination, he repeated more than anything else, he was the perpetrator of the assassination, and he said it as if he were not only saying the words but putting himself inside them in order to have been within what they were saying, as if he had immersed himself in their language to such an extent and become one with them to such a point that he could have actually been in the place where the events unfolded and even been, himself, what was done.

He must have been waiting there—he said suddenly with a look in his eyes that seemed to have no need to look in order to see everything—in the bathrooms or the hallway, just as he must have waited there before, on other days, blending in and hiding himself in the chaos of students, and he must have seen that day, like the others, that after a certain time there were fewer and fewer people left in most of the offices, and especially in the hallways, but that the professor nevertheless, like every other day, went on working all the same in his office, night already fallen, the building finally quiet, the hum, now only of the city, on the other side of the glass, all alone, as usual, in the silent light of his lamp, until the time the building would close. And when a long time had gone by without him seeing anyone, without anyone coming to his office to consult with him or talk to him about anything, and the humming of the fluorescent lights in the hall was the only sound you could hear, unless his own heart was beating, which I doubt, then it was he who approached the half-open door, who rapped on the door; *knock-knock, knock-knock*, the poor man inside would hear, and he would say come in, please come in, have a seat, don't just stand there, mostly likely without yet raising his eyes from the work he was doing—one more paragraph, one more sentence, one word to try to understand something more about the world, to try to make some order out of it. But once he felt the presence, standing in front him, of the person he'd invited in, his figure only barely lit by the desk lamp shining its light onto the open books and the loose pages he was writing on, he would raise his eyes fully and then he would see, with a shock more chilling than anything he would have ever felt in his entire life, the outline of the individual and the shadow of the pistol that were taking him at that exact moment to the next life, the flash of the gunshots, two to the chest and another, with him now slumped over his writings, to the back of the neck—two to the chest and another, with him now slumped over, to the back of the neck, he repeated—and the shadow of the eyes of that person who was my son and had decided, he or whoever it was, like a God, and at the same time like the most imbecile of fools, to take him from this world forever.

With these same words, with these same sentences that he went on shaping, polishing, and perfecting as if trying to make them worthy of emerging from an oracle's mouth, he went over the scene again and again, like someone reciting a chant. Some moments, it was true that he seemed to his son like an oracle, but other moments he just seemed like a drunk, a man fatally inebriated with guilt and pain, obsessed, perhaps with what he can see better than anyone else or perhaps with the urge to not to see anything more, precisely because he'd seen, better than anyone else, what he'd seen. But little by little, by dint of going over it again and again, his voice was beginning to crack, getting thinner, becoming ever more indistinguishable, inaudible, almost only a murmur, or a tremor.

After several hours, when exhaustion had taken as much of a toll on them as anguish, his son motioned as if to help him up from his chair and take him to bed. But at his son's first movement, it was he who quickly got up, who pushed back the chair in which he had let himself go, and once on his feet, as if he had reawakened on the way to his room, he again took up his litany. Or the other poor guy—he said—the journalist. He had been in his same old bar having his same old coffee prepared by the same old hands, he'd been breathing the same old air and hearing the same old words and seeing the same old light of that lousy day, and maybe glancing at him, brushing shoulders with him, and then at the exit, that poor man with his newspapers under his arm, and his wife and children waiting for him so they could all go somewhere because it was Sunday, that man steps out the exit and he follows him, right behind, not so close that he notices him or so far that he might get out of range, and as soon as he turns the corner onto the alleyway leading to the man's home and he sees that no one is coming, that no one is coming up ahead or behind him, that there's no one to the left or to the right, or down below or, most especially, up above, in the heavens, because there is no God whatsoever for any of these people, unless you count the grotesque ideology that passes for Him, so he goes and readies the gun in his hand, the same gun he had already used to kill the poor man working as a member of the Guardia Civil and would subsequently use to kill the professor, and he quickly lets off two shots, two shots to the back of his neck, two shots in the back, just like that, *bang, bang*, and the way the man was walking in front of him, with nothing but his newspapers in his hand and his eyes on the road, he didn't have time to see, even out of the corner of his eye, the brave specimen of a scoundrel who took his life exactly as if he were some sort of supreme judge, this petulant, sickened scoundrel who is my son and who most likely didn't even open his mouth other than to say take that, suck on this, you fucking hack, or you fucking chalk pusher, or you pansy-ass fucking pig.

Without taking off his shoes, without removing his wool sweater, which still had blotches of dirt and sap from the old cherry tree on it, and without shaking off the droning recitation that came issuing from his mouth like the rising of a river too long stagnant, he got into his bed by himself, without turning on the light or accepting the least bit of help or the slightest gesture of consolation. For a good while still, his son in the room next door could hear the man chant on, that man he'd always known as quiet, always serene, as self-possessed as a tree and as determined as an open road, the man who would often recite those lines of Calderón that his father had taught him a long time ago: "When reason's dull, the mind depressed," it went, "he best doth speak who keeps his silence best."

But after some time, which because he was half-dozing, he couldn't have said whether it was long or short, he heard him get out of bed and leave his room without making any noise.

He didn't follow him, he didn't get up to keep him company or fix him something warm to eat; he knew all too well that he wouldn't be able to offer him any relief or know how to comfort him, and that only time—solitude and time and the ability to take up his road again and go back to being who he was—could heal his wound, that deep gash in his insides, which is where, if he hoped to ever move on, he would have no other choice but to set about finding himself again, like someone who at first discovers nothing but a pin in the darkness of a room in which he can ascertain neither the dimensions of the space nor how thick the darkness might grow.

From his bed in the next room, he couldn't figure out what he was doing or where his footsteps were leading, but when suddenly he heard the great, old, solid wood door suddenly close and the bronze knocker rattle softly for a second, he knew that if he gave him something of a head start so that he could walk alone with his thoughts for a stretch, no doubt he could catch up to him somewhere along that same old road he couldn't help but go along to find himself, as if it were something inseparable from himself, so very himself, in fact, that he couldn't have gotten along without its company, just as a person can't get along without his hands or his eyes.

He knew he needed to leave him to his own devices for a bit, that he needed to leave his father alone for a little in the place where he would be sure of finding the something of himself that might have remained if not unspoiled, at least unchangeable at its core, or maybe something—something that might be his world or God or his own insides—that he could listen to or that would speak to him the way things perhaps do, rather than there being only our desire to have something speak to us.

So he figured that if he went out a bit later, in just a few minutes, he could follow him at a distance and run into him at some point or other along the road, maybe still close or maybe a little farther away from the house, but in any case walking somewhere along one of the bends in the trail. Maybe beyond the old abandoned mill, where the asphalt lane turned into a packed-earth road, or afterward, when the road turned into a bridle trail, or perhaps when the mighty mass of Pedralén came into view, or maybe even alongside the stone cross instead, directly below its highest point, beneath the circular flights of the Egyptian vultures a good part of the year, where his father's name, which was also his own as well as theirs, had been chiseled into the base. Although it might also be that if he gave him a bigger head start, he would come upon him a bit farther along, even, where the yellowish leaves of the black poplars would project onto his questions there in the early morning a feeble, almost whispered light, entirely insufficient, but at the same time primordial. Whatever pace he might walk at, there was no doubt he would come upon him at one spot or another, and when he did, he would surely find him much more collected, more as he was, with much more himself in him than the evening before. Look, Felipe, look and listen all around you, son—he seemed to be hearing—mold yourself to it, to all of it, but do it without ever setting aside your sense of wonder, that which, as incomprehensible as it may seem, embraces all things at the same time as it frees you from everything.

On their way back—he had found him alongside the stone cross, directly below the highest point of the promontory—they agreed that after lunch they would undertake a trip to Madrid to try to see Juanjo in jail as soon as possible; to see Potote, his son said, and it instantly seemed that he regretted having done so. His father would spend that night and any other nights that were necessary in the room he boarded at while at school, and he would sleep on the dining room couch, and most likely, assuming they didn't hit any snags, he would be able to see him right away.

"I'm not going to go in," his son anticipated him.

His father gave a small nod of assent; the hollows of his eyes, it seemed to him when he saw him nod, were like two henbane flowers, their dark purple depths branching out in subtle, violet venations around the yellowish corollas.

18

When he got there, he went directly over and sat down in one of the chairs positioned in front of the glass partition that divided the room in half. The glass was thick, double-pane, and it went from your waist up to a yard or so from the ceiling, and beyond his own image reflected in it, there was nothing but a white wall, with no decoration or furnishings, at the center of which was a completely smooth, closed, metal door. Above the door, an enormous, round wall clock presided, like those old religious symbols, over the entire halved space. He couldn't hear it, but it nevertheless seemed to be the only thing, apart from the hum of the fluorescent lights, which he could easily imagine as being a dialectic synthesis of its ticking, that there was to perceive in the emptiness of the room.

There weren't any people, either, on the other side of the glass or behind him, only twin metal doors sealed so perfectly tight that not the least sound could get through nor the slightest movement be discerned behind them, and more than imprisoning space, you might say that what they were detaining was, strictly speaking, time. Felipe looked at the wall, the blank, white wall in front of him, but the only thing he could see was the reflection in the double-pane glass of his own image superimposed on the perfectly visible movements of the clock's ticking hands. With an instinctive motion, he moved his head from side to side, and the image of his face, his full, broad face covered all over with wrinkles, coincided exactly with the face of the clock. Tick-tock, he then seemed to hear with acute precision.

As if what he was awaiting were the execution of his death sentence, droplets of memories floated up into his mind, crisscrossing it with no rhyme or reason, as they say happens to the dying just before they pass. Neither the sure victory of oblivion nor the will to banish them seemed in the least able to stand against the unstoppable, growing force with which they emerged, and the images continued to imprint themselves on the glass of his memory, just like his reflection on the thick, double-pane glass that divided the room in half, even though what he saw in one was fixed and blurry, a fractioning, even, of the image in the double layer of glass, and in the other there was nothing but swiftness and clarity.

He saw the beginnings of the storm that first day he went back home from the field after his return to the village, less than a year ago, and of the one that last day before his departure from it; he saw the years spent along the road with the metalworks and the tire retread shop after that, and the dining room in his apartment, where the furniture was so garish it seemed to be arguing with whoever was using it and where he spent ever more time in his corner next to the window. He saw Asunción, he saw her increasingly incomprehensible expression, increasingly dry and disconnected from the things that had been theirs, and her face, too, so long ago, on the day they'd coated themselves with mud beneath the poplar trees by the river, the day they liked to think, because of how happy they'd been, and even though the dates didn't work out right, that the two of them had conceived the son he was now waiting to appear on the other side of the glass. And suddenly he saw—he was still a little boy, a whelp no more than three feet high— the eyes of his father, may he rest in peace, the serene and resignedly melancholic eyes of his father—Felipe Díaz, like him, Felipe Díaz Díaz—on the desolate night when they burst violently into the house, when they virtually broke down the door, his mother would say when she told the story, those little men in blue shirts from who knows where, and it doesn't really matter, anyway. Four or five boys, they were no more than boys—his mother narrated, because even though you can forgive and forget, my son, you should never forget, she would say—four or five boys under the orders of one of those brazen thugs who have always existed and will always exist in this loathsome world, make no mistake, but whom certain circumstances allow to do whatever they please and even to dictate the lives and deaths of others, although other circumstances, at least, do not. Those years, Felipe, my son, his mother would continue, always using almost the exact same words each time she told the story, they were the first kind of circumstances, years when even the biggest nitwit could fill his mouth with grand words that masked nothing more than wickedness and villainy, wickedness and villainy all around, she would always repeat. It seemed as if all the stupidity and arrogance combined and all the vanity in the world had gone to the heads of most everyone, and that all those of ill will, who, of course, called themselves by a different name, using appealing, almost pretty language—and those of good will right behind them, imagine that, or out in front of them, make no mistake, like little, euphoric sheep— had gotten together and made a pact to call the shots everywhere. Like Abelardo, remember him? Abelardo

García Quiñones, the man with the field next to ours, in that spot where his sons would later plant nothing but poplars and then more poplars, and so it pleased God—his mother would always add at this point, as if hoping it would serve as a warning or a reminder, more than a mere, useless indulgence—to call him to account, right then and there.

He saw his father's eyes—he heard his mother's voice—and he saw, too, the shiny boots, the buckles, the intruders' glistening leather jackets on that dazzling night, and more than anything he saw their guns and he saw their expressions, which now, so many years later, were still as overlapping as his reflection in that glass that divided the room in half. The boastfulness of the revolvers, he thought, the boastfulness of the revolvers and the fatuous braggadocio of their haughty, disdainful expressions, and now there rose up again to imprint themselves on his memory those furious, contemptuous, cocksure smiles that he'd spent his whole life trying to run away from, that he would have given anything to be able to bury once and for all in oblivion, but whose lurking image, apparently no matter how much time passed or how hard he tried to avoid it, he seemed to be condemned, like someone condemned to some sort of life sentence, to witness. Because he knew that just as others are pursued their whole lives by bad luck or disease or the inability to match their strength to what needs to be done, his sentence, his real leap in the dark, which he had already taken, was the oppressiveness of that impertinent, smug glow, the black glow of malice and imbecility in the smiles of those who arrogate to themselves absolute power over the lives of others and act with treacherous superiority upon the deserted defenselessness of others.

And now he saw that glow again, now he saw it again at the same time as he saw, alternating with it, the eyes of his father, so tall, gaunt, erect and yet at the same time such a small thing on the threshold of the doorway between the kitchen and the patio. The breeze—he remembered as if it were yesterday—made the leaves tremble on the cherry tree, whose fruit they had recently picked, and his father, may he rest in peace, told them that they could look wherever they wanted, but they weren't going to find anyone there.

"Look, Felipe, you're playing with fire here, I know you have that anarchist vermin around here somewhere, and you really are playing with fire. So I hope you know what you're doing."

"All I know, Abelardo, is that the person you're calling a vermin of whatever sort—and I don't really care about any of that and I never have—is a good man and an honest man through and through, incapable of doing anyone wrong, no matter what, and as a worker, and you know this better than anybody, he's second to none. That's what I know, and you know it, too."

"Felipe, Felipe, I'm telling you, you're playing with fire here, don't push your luck now, just tell us where you're hiding him, because in the end we'll find him, and then where he goes, you'll go, too, head first. Felipe, think about your wife and your son."

"That's what I'm doing, Abelardo, and I'm wondering if you're doing the same."

They took him. My mother, your grandmother—he told his son as they traveled in the train to Madrid—went out after them, screaming like a madwoman and clutching at Abelardo's jacket, at Abelardo, our neighbor, the owner of the plot next to ours, where the poplars are now, pleading with him by all that he held dear to not hurt him, it was Felipe, Felipe, his neighbor, a man he'd known his whole life.

I'd stayed behind with my aunts and uncles next to the open door, he went on, I was crying and crying as hard as I could from seeing my mother screaming like that, and through my tears I saw her lying on the ground, lying there but still shouting, with her arm outstretched in the direction they were taking him, before she, too, broke into a fit of sobbing I will remember the rest of my life.

I quickly jumped from my uncle's arms—he'd been restraining me as best he could—and I went running to her. I don't know how the word could have popped into my head or where I'd gotten it from, I must have been barely nine years old, but I said it, shouted it, rather, or I shouted it at them before bursting into tears again, because my aunt had sped straight after me and slapped her hand over my mouth. Murderers, I shouted, murderers, and the whole village, hidden behind half-closed shutters and barely-cracked balcony doors, heard it and will always remember it. The child who called them by their true name, they said.

Since then, he continued, I think I've always had that hand of my aunt's covering my mouth, and that unspoken desire to break into a run and shout all the things that are exactly what words sometimes say they are. But at the same time, and above all, what I've also always had, what has always been with me, what has never stopped stalking me, hounding me, without my being able to undo the ties that bind me to it always, constantly, without a moment's peace, without being able to look behind me or ahead of me, or outside, or even, would you believe, inside my own house, is that dread, that dread like a deer caught in the glow of a smile I think I can recognize as clearly as a metal detector locates ancient coins or spear tips under a layer of earth. A fear whose snake I have, perhaps as a result of wanting so badly to run away from it all and pretend like it had nothing to do with me, allowed to hatch from within my very insides.

What happened next? What happened next you already know, he went on telling his son on the train. Paco, the Straightedge—that's what they nicknamed him, because he couldn't live with even a single crooked furrow and would drive the plowshare back in again and again and as many times as it took for it to come out as straight as he wanted it, that was the man's obsession—was found in a sort of low cellar, very well hidden, that my father, your grandfather, had made for him under the shed in the field, which now just holds a bunch of old junk. They turned everything inside out, they took some of the baled hay and burned it there in the dead of night to light up the area, it must have made one devil of a pyre, until they finally found the hideout. They must have exchanged some words there, although nobody can know what was said, and then they took him and my father, may he rest in peace, back along the road.

At the spot where you can turn and go down to where the henbanes grow, but on the opposite side, if you've noticed, there's a path that goes up the hillside. I've never taken it, but if you follow it, after about an hour of walking you'll come to the top of Pedralén. That's the path they turned off onto, and when they got to the top, at the very highest point of the promontory, and it had to have been first light by then, they set them up at the edge of the cliff, and with no further ado they started tossing them off, one by one, the two of them—Paco and my father—and three other poor, unfortunate souls they had brought up from the village. Those are the names chiseled on that cross they put up in '77, the names of those four people and your grandfather, whose name is the same as mine.

He didn't say *mine and yours*, he only said *mine*, and then he spent practically the rest of the trip in silence, as if his aunt had slapped her hand over his mouth again.

19

After a time, a time that, despite its sitting there right in front of his eyes, ticking itself out on the clock in the perfectly appreciable movements of its two hands, he wouldn't have been able to say at first whether it felt infinite or was perhaps just a single instant drawn completely out or perhaps contracted to its smallest possible expression, Felipe Díaz Carrión saw the door in the middle of the wall before him open, and immediately afterward there came a pair of guards who each instantly took up a post to either side of the door, followed by a pair of off-white sneakers poking out from under the somewhat frayed hems of a pair of worn jeans. He watched the sneakers come in, he watched them approach the other side of the glass in which his own image was reflected, but he suddenly lacked the courage to raise his eyes, to impart even the slightest movement to his eyelids that would allow him to finally look him in the face and see his eyes, in case they now had, or, rather, still had, that expression that had been haunting him an entire lifetime, making it impossible for him to erase it from his imagination or get a moment's peace, that expression that emerged from the past and had returned to hem in the present and was not simply presumptuousness or disdain, nor merely annoyance or defiance, but instead, and in addition to all that, disgust, rancor, bitter repugnance, and foolish repulsion, all crowning the grotesque emptiness of what they cruelly believed to be not only beyond good and evil but beyond any single limit, as confusing or changeable or skittish as it might be.

"What's this? You don't even have the guts to look at me, or what, you halfwit?" his son spat at him suddenly.

And then, gradually, as if that slight movement of eyelids required an enormous dose of an energy that he would never be able to fully muster, he raised his eyes, he lifted them little by little from the spot where the sneakers he saw come in were, although he could no longer see them, up to the worn jeans, then to the belt buckle, and the wool sweater, and when he finally got to his eyes, but even before then, in the angle of his chin, the sneer on his lips, he knew what he had perhaps never stopped knowing, no matter how much he might have wished not to know or believed he didn't— namely, that there was nothing to be done, there was no possible way out and no going back, regardless of how little he was able to explain it to himself or perhaps even admit it to himself, and that by virtue of all that, and by virtue of all that was at stake for him, he was irredeemably condemned.

His image in the glass that halved the room where it seemed only time alone dwelt was superimposed on that of his son, his resigned, melancholic expression superimposed on the other's dismissive repugnance, which was now, once again, opening its mouth and, with fingers interlaced in a gesture that had already been engraved on his memory—"What's with you? Cat got your tongue?" he'd said to him—mockingly inquiring whether he wasn't going to dish him out one of his bullshit, preachy, hopelessly fascist spiels.

"You're such a coward and such a nobody," he burst out, "that you don't even have the guts to speak. That's what you've always been, a nobody, an absolute nothing, do you hear me? A fucking dried-out, squashed old turd sitting there in the middle of that stupid road you love so much, a dirt-poor nonentity who has no place in this world and has never had the least idea about anything. Didn't you come here to talk? So talk, goddammit, say something!"

There were a lot of things he would have liked to say, or perhaps the only thing he could have done would have been to say a lot of things, to explain to him once again, for instance, that each of us sees and thinks in his own way—or at least that's what he believes—but that that doesn't change the fact that as much as a person might like what he thinks, or as fond as he may be of what he's dreamt up, or as confident or convinced as he may be that he's right or in the right—and you can always convince yourself of whatever you like and for whatever reason—other people aren't under the least obligation to think like he thinks or want what he wants, nor does that person have the right to any such a thing, much less any kind of right that could be labeled with one of those grand, pretty words that a lot of people use as a mantle to hide those most broken-down of ideas they're peddling; and that a person can do whatever he wants, of course, but not just whatever he feels like, because then he will have to answer for it personally. And after that, he would have liked to say, or perhaps would have only been able to say, do you understand me? Do you understand me now, my son?

But it was no longer really that, and it no longer had anything really to do with that, nor could it—at this point he couldn't even nag him—and apart from looking into a pair of eyes and assuring himself of their expression, the only thing he had really come to do was to say to him what have you done. What have you done, my son? Do you understand? Do you understand that you've killed someone? That you've taken the lives of several men? Do you understand that? Tell me, tell me if you're capable of actually thinking about what you've done, if you have the freedom, that word you all use so much, to be able to truly think about what you've done. You've taken a man's life; the thing I raised, the life I produced, has suddenly resolved to take the lives of other people who, for whatever confounded reason, he has decided to consider not as people but as things, burdens, obstacles, abstractions. How could you do it? How is it possible that a son of mine, who is—and let me just say this—flesh of my flesh, blood of my blood, or at any rate is at least my handiwork, has been able to go to such lengths of imbecility? Which is what evil is, first and foremost—pure, completely idiotic imbecility. What did I do wrong, tell me, what must I have done wrong? What part of this is my fault?

But he couldn't, or perhaps wouldn't, say anything, or rather he wasn't able to articulate a single word out loud. He just looked at him, looked at him the way you look at an image that you have done nothing but look at with fear your entire life and try to run from, to scare off, to shoo away as you might shoo a horsefly or a persistent, insistent bumblebee. It had seemed to him that if he attempted to speak a word, he wouldn't know how to pronounce it, that it wouldn't actually come out, and that even if it did, even if he was, in the end, able to pronounce it and then go on to articulate even whole sentences, even possibly those same sentences he had uttered other times before, he wouldn't actually be able to make himself understood, because things could no longer be said in the same way, or words no longer meant the same things, they couldn't be modulated or put together the same way as before, as if something in their relationship, in the way they were strung together or made to follow on one another, or in their way of being stitched or assigned to things, something in their gift for expression, you might go so far as to think, had become so jumbled and muddled that words no longer meant what they said and no longer made of things what they were. They were no longer enough—it seemed to him—neither of them were, because words no longer linked him to things or brought them closer to him, they only snatched things from him and moved them farther away. Something had wormed its way into them and hollowed them out, or wormed its way into our way of saying them, he thought, some central beam had become so utterly rotten that there was no longer any firm surface upon which to stand that wouldn't have collapsed, and now nothing he might say, assuming he ever managed to be able to say it, could come anywhere close to saying what things were and what it was he felt, or even to simply making himself understood as he would have liked to be. Because on top of it all, words, too, whether we like it or not, have, and always have had, it's true, their own other side of the glass, and it might be that the only thing that could get there was their mirror image, the empty profile or the hollow shell of their sound, which might now elicit nothing more than mocking or derision from him.

So he got up, he got up from the chair in front of the glass partition that divided the room in half; he was totally exhausted, which was surprising for someone who had done nothing but sit there silently, and after confirming once more, in a final attempt to look at him, that at no point, at no blasted point, not at the beginning, when he first saw him, not for the entire time he had been there—and he couldn't have said if the time had been long or short, fleeting as the blink of an eye or completely endless—and not even now, when he saw the end was fast approaching, at not a single, blasted, infernal moment had his son even come close to removing that same old expression of smug self-importance and disgusted rancor in his eyes, after confirming once more what there had most likely been no need to confirm, he turned his back to him, looked straight ahead, at the door, and headed slowly for the exit.

"A whole lot of fuss over some fucking pig!" he jumped up and shouted. "Over some fucking chalk pusher, over some two-bit hack just as full of shit as you are, you fucking pussy, you fucking nobody, you're a nobody and a fascist and you always will be!" And at the same time he was spouting off these words, as if he had never in his life said any other words and nothing had ever meant anything other than what he was saying, he suddenly began, with an intensity of violence accentuated by the suddenness of his outburst, to pound on the glass partition that divided the room in half and through which the image of his father's back was gradually disappearing.

It couldn't have taken more than a few seconds for his father, impassive, to cover the half dozen yards that separated him from the exit and turn the handle to pull open the metal slab of a door, the same amount of seconds it took the pair of guards posted under the clock to get to his son and subdue him, one on each side, holding to neutralize him. But it was likewise an infinite world of time, with its thick glass in which everything was reflected twofold into a vortex of images, that definitively separated time itself into two and the world into two and perhaps even, if such a thing were possible, the infinite or the definitive into two. Will the same thing happen at the end, will we not know if life has slipped away from us in the blink of an eye or if it dragged on eternally, he would later wonder.

They dragged him away toward the metal door in the middle of the room while he continued shouting at the top of his lungs you piece-of-shit traitor and you fucking piece-of-shit father, crawl back to that shithole of yours you should've never come out of in the first place and I hope you rot there more than you've ever rotted anywhere in your entire fucking piece-of-shit life.

They immediately yanked him out, his father had slowly disappeared through the other door, as well, and nothing remained but time, ticking itself out and persisting unopposed—the shouts he continued to hurl from the other side weren't coming through now, not even muffled—as the sole presence in that empty space.

20

His younger son saw him push against the door's glass pane and, once outside the imposing edifice, after taking the three or four steps that seemed to use up the last remaining inertia of his exit, suddenly pull up and stop short, spiritless and tiny in the distance, not knowing what direction to point his feet and not even realizing he didn't know. He looked up, at the blue of the sky, at the rows of identical windows on the apartment buildings, and then all around him, at the views of streets crisscrossed by cars, cars, and more cars, all going in opposite directions, and people hurrying in and out of the same door he had just left through but not exactly left behind. Lost, his son Felipe said to himself, watching him from the window of the bar where they had arranged to meet, the poor man is completely lost, he has no idea which way to turn or which way to look, and broken, he said to himself, his heart has been broken.

In the middle of all of that coming and going of people who were going about their business and knew where they were going, he now seemed to have nothing at all to go about but the literal ground on which he was walking, and his next step forward. That was his road now—his single next step forward, he thought. And he went on watching him take short, tentative steps as if he might, after each one, regret having taken it or even topple over a cliff, then stop again like some halfwit and try to look up, only to immediately look down at the ground again, as if wanting to ask it something, or rather evaluate something, or perhaps just needing to have something to assure himself of his own presence. It's as if before he takes a step, he needs to say goodbye to the previous one, he thought.

When he finally made up his mind to start walking in the direction he couldn't help but walk in, it seemed to his son that it took him a yeoman's effort—as his father was in the habit of saying—to descend the one dozen steps that separated that official building from the sidewalk and head toward him. It seemed like he had to request permission from one foot to put the other one forward, and that once on the sidewalk, it took him not just an interminable but an incomprehensible amount of time to walk across the crosswalk, agonizing the vehicles that now had a green light.

Several times, he was on the verge of running out of the bar where he had been waiting and going to take him by the arm, to say Dad, I'm here, or it's just here, this is where we're going, but a paralysis akin to that which had taken over his father seemed to have seized him, as well. So just as he had been watching, up until only a moment ago, the foam dissolving in his glass of beer, he watched him from behind the bar window come slowly toward him; he watched him cross the street, as a person crosses a rope bridge suspended from one side of a chasm to the other, and then stop again at the door to check for something that couldn't possibly be missed, and afterward, but only after a before that did not now seem to retain any connection to its after, come in with an air of clumsiness and disorientation that were truly unprecedented in his father. It seemed that he had returned from those just barely two hours, which is how long it took, what with one thing and another, with an additional twenty years on him.

The bar was small, two windows onto the street and fewer than a dozen tables, and there was no one there right then but him and the waiter puttering around behind the bar, but despite all that, he had to catch his eye, like someone trying to make out something from a distance or pick someone out of a crowd. I'm here, Dad, he felt the need to say, it's me, Felipe.

He pushed the beer bottles that had been accumulating on the table to one side and asked him what he wanted to drink. Nothing, nothing, there's nothing there, he answered everything without him needing to make a second enquiry. You were smart to stay here.

He wanted to go back to the village that very same day, he couldn't be tempted by any of the suggestions his son had put forward for spending the rest of the day together in Madrid, and they got home late into the night. The following morning, he again found him under the cherry tree out on the patio. He was stiff with cold, huddled in an odd position and still wearing his good jacket, which he hadn't bothered to take off, curled up and clutching the tree trunk. Cowering like a dog, his son thought. His cheek was covered in scrapes again, and the dried blood on the scratches in the stubble along his jawline made the paleness of his face stand out even more.

He picked him up—geez, Dad, was all he could think to say to him—and he took him in to the bathroom. Then, once he made sure he was cleaned up and, as far as he could tell, calm, he went out to buy a loaf of bread, and when he got back, he made him a large, black coffee, just the way he liked it, along with his nice, thick slices of bread and some of the thyme and Spanish lavender honey a neighbor gathered every year, a neighbor from a family that had the first and last names of one of their own listed just above his father's on the cross at Pedralén.

They didn't speak, they couldn't or didn't feel like speaking, except about specific, mundane things they were doing or had right in front of them, so they each concentrated on their own coffee, just as he, the day before, had concentrated on watching his beer foam dissolving—the head, his father had told him a long time ago, the foam on a beer is called the *head*, just as *cachaza* is the foam that forms on the top of cane juice, and I suppose that's where *cachazudo* comes from, calm like foam.

What dissolves like foam, he thought, or he might have thought the day before, what vanishes calmly, disappearing unperturbed, as slowly and peacefully as foam when it fades away, and also just the opposite, what is suddenly lost, what is erased in an instant, what we were used to having exist and be important or even crucial for us, whether we knew it or not, suddenly, without our even coming to completely realize it, it all

139

falls off a cliff and disappears. Like the meaning that binds us to things, that reassures us and encourages us and signals to us from within things but then one day, before we've had enough time to even know what it was or what it truly consisted of, suddenly collapses or simply disappears off a dark cliff at the bottom of which there now remains only its carcass, its neck broken, at the mercy of the unsparing pecking of the great vultures of the void—the black vultures or the griffon vultures or the bearded vultures of senselessness—or any elegant, white Egyptian vulture that might swoop down and make off with its eyes.

He was scared for his father, he pitied him, but on the other hand he couldn't bear to feel that way, nor could he resign himself to the fact that the calm strength he had always admired in his father, his quiet valor, had also masked an allotment of fear and a measure of humiliation and that it could all, from one moment to the next, come crashing so spectacularly down. One day, two nights after their arrival from Madrid, he came upon him rifling nervously through one of the drawers in the sideboard. Finally he pulled out a large, tin box stuffed to the seams with old photographs— photographs of his father (his own grandfather), and of his father and mother together, and also of him and the rest of the family, and friends of the family. Photographs of the two of them, as well, of him and Asun, and of little Juanjo when they still lived in the village.

He shuffled through them all, he looked at all of them, and afterward he slowly picked out all the ones with Juanjo in them, from the time he was born up until when he must have been about ten, when they emigrated to the north. He placed them all next to each other in a row on the table, and then he set about examining them one by one; he peered closely at them, he would pause at each one for the same not so much interminably as incomprehensibly long amount of time as he'd seen through the bar window that it took him to walk across the crosswalk, and then he would set them back down again in the exact same spot before picking up the one next to it and spending the same amount of time contemplating that one.

"You see?" he said to him after more than an hour of ignoring him completely. "You see how it's not him? You see how he doesn't have even close to the same look on his face?"

When he said that to him, he held one of the photographs in his hand as if brandishing it at him or offering it to him, and then he took it with him into his room.

The following morning, when he heard him get up to wash, during one of the few, brief moments he let it out of his sight, Felipe went into his room to look at it.

He didn't recall ever having seen it before. It was a portrait of his father on the day of the village's autumn feast day, according to the caption on the back, photographed from the waist up alongside his firstborn son. He was dressed very elegantly, with that look of health and robustness he'd had before he began to grow thin just a few years later, and both his hands were gripping the handlebars of a bicycle, while the young boy sat on the crossbar. Judging by his apparent age, eight or nine at the most, it must have been taken one of the years immediately preceding their departure from the village. Juanjo was wearing a little, peaked cap to protect him from the sun, and a wool sweater, and in his clasped hands he held a bunch of daisies that looked just picked. His expression—his little smile somewhere between shy and surprised at the photographer—was alert, pleasant, lively, and bright, and it poked out right at the top of the bouquet of flowers he held clasped in his hands at the very center of the handlebars.

His father's wide, round face, with his abundant hair combed straight back and his full mustache and eyebrows—his few, lone hairs, as Asunción used to joke—had the same sure, melancholic expression he'd always seen on him.

"Those clasped little hands!" he said when he returned from the bathroom and caught him staring at the photograph. "Those clasped little hands, Felipe!"

The days went by one after another as they ate breakfast in silence and ate dinner in silence, as if, most of the time, words had flown off to some foreign land covered in the carcasses of signs and the cadavers of sentences, carrion even before it was dead, as they went out for walks in silence, with the exasperating slowness of someone suffering from a recent bout of rheumatism or else afflicted by an unexpected paralysis, until one night at the end of two weeks— he seemed to get on well enough now at the village club, listening to the news, which he still called the newscast, from a seat in the corner and watching several of his friends play cards—his son told him he had to go back to Madrid, that he couldn't stay with him any longer.

"You've already been here too long, Felipe, my son. Go, go ahead, son."

Every time he said anything to him those last several days, even something insignificant or some isolated detail, he would add that on like a grace note—*son, my son*. He's holding on, he thought, he's holding on to that tagline as if clutching at straws to find some way for the meaning of the words he's saying to not slip away. Or maybe as if it were his final foothold, a lone toehold for him to cling to so as not to fall off the cliff.

He hadn't wanted to return to the road that led to the field, and that seemed strange to him, though, on the other hand, he had watched him sitting calmly in front of the television down at the club and then linger a good while longer, standing there and eagerly following the card game in which his neighbor who brought him the honey always played. He's getting on well enough, he thought. But one afternoon he realized that when he followed the games, more than paying attention to the players' decisions, he was keeping track of the cards each of them received, to the tricks they had taken rather than what they did with them, and also that instead of watching whatever was being shown on the television, he seemed in fact to be seeing some sort of reflection on the screen, as if it were merely glass; he afterward thought, nevertheless, that time, in any case, would make time for itself, as it always does, and that everything would continue along its course, as it was meant to and as it usually did.

When the sun set the following day, a calm day in November, after they'd had dinner together, he finally said goodbye. The pomegranates behind the old mill must be ripe by now, he said to him as he took his leave, knowing how happy it always made him when that particular fruit ripened and cracked open; when I get back, and I'll come back as soon as I can, we'll go pick some.

But two days later, he woke up very early, having been unsettled by a strange dream. Several bales of hay were burning in the night, shooting up towering flames that seemed intent on burning everything; now they were licking the walls of the house he was in, and above him were the white silhouettes of birds he feared might swoop down on him at any moment. But that wasn't the worst of it, the worst was instead a muffled, resounding sound, like someone shaking out a blanket, or a gigantic drop falling, like a dead weight, with a smothered sound onto a thick layer of dust laid down over months and months of drought. The crackling fire, rather than illuminating anything, impeded his view of what was happening beyond and, especially, his ability to hear anything or figure out what direction the sound was coming from, but he went on straining and straining to hear, until the fire ignited the poplars and the conflagration that then ensued finally overwhelmed him, preventing him from hearing the slightest sound other than the noise of everything being consumed.

As he took his first sip of the coffee he had just prepared, large and black, just like his father took it, he recalled again that over the course of the weeks he'd spent with him after their return from Madrid, he hadn't ventured out to the field even once. So he tossed back his coffee—he saw his dream again—grabbed his jacket, and without even waiting for the elevator, he took off running down the stairs and didn't stop until he reached the car.

When he arrived hours later and opened the great, old door with the bronze knocker, his father wasn't there anymore. He hadn't had breakfast, and his bed hadn't been slept in; there was only a pencil and a completely blank sheet of paper—with a few dots grouped in the upper left—sitting on the clean kitchen table.

Without wasting a second, he took the car as far as he could, until he got to the exact place where the packed-earth road stopped being fit for anything other than a person on foot, where just past the spot where the pomegranate trees stuck out, a path descended down to where the henbane grew and another, almost directly across the road from it, gradually ascended, crossing gullies and thyme plants, to the top of Pedralén. An hour, he remembered his having told him, one hour, more or less, under normal conditions. He didn't even shut the car door after pulling up to a sudden halt, he just stepped out into the giant dust cloud he'd kicked up and blasted off running, first along the road and then up the mountain, without losing a single instant.

He was gasping for breath, his heart was exploding, sometimes he ran and other times he climbed in great strides, huffing and puffing. Still in the distance, on the crest of the promontory, he spotted him. He was on the edge, at the highest point, directly above the modest cross hewn from the same limestone as the mountain itself and on whose base, also made out of the same stone, was chiseled, alongside four other names, the name of his father, which was also his own.

21

Debilitated, as if burdened by a weight greater than anything he had ever borne in his entire life, you might even say incapacitated or crippled, Felipe Díaz—Felipe Díaz Carrión—had finally managed that autumn morning to reach the top, on that path that weaved among boulders and crags and wound its way up the steep pitch.

Stopping every so often, inhaling sharply once and then again and then quickly beginning his trek again, he had climbed, without ever quite catching his breath completely or taking his eyes off the ground, off the pebbles he was crunching beneath his feet or the clumps of grass he was trampling, the thistles and gorse he swerved around more out of habit than for any other reason, or above all off the ground, the sere, dusty earth that it seemed to him he had done nothing in his life but walk upon, with feet increasingly just as cracked and dry as the earth itself, but more than anything, he never stopped looking at what he was looking at, he kept his eyes (might he have said facing head-on, or was it more like his final humiliation?) on that which he had focused them on indelibly—the unyielding, omnipresent expression that no matter where he looked, whether all around him or forward or backward in time, was now the only thing he could see and the only thing pulling him on, like a lead rope, the only thing that spurred him on, with a reverberation that caused everything around it that was not it and was not born of it to wilt, reducing it to a single glow, a single, fixed point, polished and sharpened to the absolute limit, on which everything hung and everything was held fast.

At the right time, he kept saying to himself, at the right time, when I could begin to sense which way the wind was blowing, as he puts it, that's when I should have given him a nice, big piece of my mind, when I could have done it and I didn't, or I didn't think I had to, and when I could have seen it coming but still didn't see it, or maybe it's just that I didn't want to.

Just who do you think you are, I should have told him, who do you think you are, although perhaps not in that tone of voice, not in that tone but in some other one, I don't know, maybe more understanding, more putting myself in his shoes, trying to reason with him and see things from his point of view, to see what he was seeing.

You've been hanging around with whoever you've been hanging around with, he could have said to him, and that's your business; you'll have seen or they'll have told you this, that, and the other thing, but when it comes to knowing, really knowing, knowing what's what, as they say, you haven't got a clue, my son, not a single clue. When it comes to feeling true concern or any sort of an inkling of real trembling in the face of people and things, and a sense of respect for the words used to talk about people and things, you haven't got a clue. You go on all day long about enemies, about the people, about oppression, about history, and about war, about suffering, about them and our own. To sublimate, isn't that the word you're always using? Well that's all it is, a sublimation of those prickings of conscience we all have and an obsession with continually twisting things around and fucking everything up. There are always a lot of messed up things in this world, son, I should have told him, a lot, and some are even worse, as your grandfather used to say, but as bad as things are, they can always get much worse still if you try to fix them by meddling around with stuff that's better left alone, if you try to go down some road you think is a wonderful shortcut and it turns out it's not a shortcut or even a road and it doesn't take you anywhere except maybe, eventually, straight off a cliff.

But he would have burst out laughing, he said to himself, he would probably have burst out laughing regardless of when I might have told him or what sort of tone I might have used, he would have just laughed and insulted me. When does a light capable of blinding everyone inside a house, and then everyone else, begin to glow, and what are its symptoms and its conditions? Is it all just chance, the paucity of what one has, the sheer power of bewitchment? And what kind of dawn is that, he went on wondering, stubbornly dissecting the question, tethering his ascent to a ballast heavier than any other possible load.

Of course, he could have called the police at the very outset, he said to himself; but how could anyone report his own son, and for what, so early on? This kid is an idiot, he could have told the cops, this kid is an idiot, but it's better to nip it in the bud before it goes any further and he turns into something else. But how could anyone report someone for being an idiot? How could anyone ever report his own son for being an idiot, or tell God that this whole thing is grotesque, that's it's not even tragic but grotesque—foolish, grotesque rancor and defiance.

Like someone who goes around and around in his thoughts and continues to weigh himself down with the impossible burden of what could have been but wasn't, Felipe Díaz slowly dragged his limbs, numbed by a feeling of guilt he was unable to dispel and petrified by the lactic acid that shot through that look, that rare, obsessive glow of a single image, fixed before his eyes, that was superimposed with overwhelming arrogance on the glass behind which the land and the plants of that exhausting ascent, and also the impeccable blue of the sky, lay apart. But as it got to about noon, when everything was so still it seemed almost as if not even silence itself could be heard up there, Felipe Díaz finally reached the highest pinnacle on the rocky crest of Pedralén.

He had never gone up there before—his shadow coincided almost exactly with the small space taken up by his feet—and he had never wanted to; he had always simply passed by, just as he had with most other things in life, come to that, at the foot of the immense rock he walked the entire length of and where he often looked upward from directly beneath the highest point of the pinnacle. He would look at that sort of small apex at the summit, where he was now standing, and he would also look at the nests of the Egyptian vultures, their gliding, their soaring—the soft parts, he recalled, the soft parts, like the eyes and the tongue—and then he would hear the voice describing what he was seeing, and even when it was seeing the worst, it described it nevertheless without bitterness or malice or resentful malevolence, exactly, but, at most, with a sort of quiet indignation or resigned hostility, a sort of impenetrable melancholy and pure, and therefore inexhaustible and perhaps even cheerful, sadness.

What could anyone possibly have against simplicity, he had wondered to himself on other occasions. What is it that makes the infinite splendor of simplicity and the roaring of the incipient storm that always follows it, if you're out to see it, go so unnoticed? What blindness isn't making a killing? But what he was wondering now and what was pounding away inside his head as he dragged himself up the mountain, practically gasping for air, was something quite different—namely, whether being such a small thing, whether having remained such a small thing, whether not having been important enough when it was necessary to be so, or being so generally unimportant were things one could be guilty of, whether his having been nothing—nothing, it echoed in his head, nothing at all, do you hear me, a fucking dried-out, squashed old turd sitting there in the middle of the road, a dirt-poor nonentity who has no place in this world—were in fact something to be guilty of, and his not having reacted or acted or taken the initiative, his not having spoken up and raised his voice and fought enough, made him somehow just as guilty as his son. As guilty as someone who had narrowed his gaze to a single, rigid, abstract point of things that eclipsed everything else, leaving them on the outside, like strangers, like enemies, of that never ending, forever changing interplay of perspectives that allows all things to be seen, and from that single viewpoint, with that unwavering fixedness and that sole perspective, he had pointed the barrel of his gun with the homicidal simplicity of a metallic hollowness that had spent years rattling and bouncing and rolling around, back and forth, as only emptiness can rattle and roll.

Didn't you come here to talk?—he couldn't help hearing the words echo in his head as he huffed his way upward—so talk, goddammit, say something, you pitiful nonentity, you have no place in this world and you'll never have any fucking place in it your whole goddamn life!

Now he was going to have a talk with him, he was thinking, now he was going to have a talk with him, just the two of them, or maybe with her, too, or who knows who else; but even then he was only going to talk to them in his own way, wordlessly, silent like raindrops before a storm, those giant, fat raindrops that pound into the dust, but with facts—or would they just be names again?—with the facts that always, each time you recall them or speak them aloud, albeit softly, sound the same and mean the same thing, limitless in their simplicity.

22

Among the talk going around the village about that dawn a few days after the beginning of the war when his father and his four other unlucky companions in misfortune were thrown from the top of that cliff, the news spread that one of them, a boy of barely twenty, had started to shout and cry so despairingly that you could hear him all the way over in the village, and that they'd amused themselves by shooting, there at the very edge of the cliff itself, at the feet of another of them—anarchist scum, they continued to call him to the last—who had surprisingly, according to the word on the street, fallen to praying. All right, one of them must have said sarcastically, let's see if you can finally make a nice, straight line now on your way down. But there didn't seem to be much of a consensus, as far as he had heard, regarding his father.

Some said he was praying to himself the entire time as they went along the road; others said that at one point during the ascent, aided by the low light, he had somehow managed to loose the bonds on his wrists and had tried to grab one of the squadron member's pistols. But the only thing they all agreed on was that Felipe Díaz, Felipe Díaz Díaz, said nothing at all in the end; all he did was to look at them, to look at each one of them with an expression of desolate sadness, and then he looked from that tall perch at all the space stretching out in every direction, and with all of that in his eyes—dawn was just beginning to break, according to what everyone had always said—they must have simply tossed him off the cliff.

He recalled this, and he then he stopped looking at the cross he had been looking at, so small down there below him, and instead he, too, slowly raised his eyes up from the edge of the crag and out onto his immense surroundings. He was still gulping in air from his climb, and his legs, numbed, or you might also say petrified, just like that mound of stone, were shaking. But after few moments, unexpectedly, as soon as he took in the vastness whose view his vantage point allowed him to command, he felt instantly secure, strangely secure, as if he were resting upon or being held up by all that immensity more than by the narrow strip of rock on which he was standing.

It was fair to say that apart from the passengers who had left their cars parked on the other side of the river in the places where the highway opened out and had stepped outside with their binoculars to admire the elegant flights of the Egyptian vultures, even during one of the months when the birds had emigrated to their winter quarters, there wasn't another soul around. Perhaps, with nothing else to see, they were now watching him; in fact, he was practically sure of it, judging by the way two of those tiny little dots were motioning wildly. But he looked away from them, from the ridiculous vanity of their movements and their concern for him (didn't they, too, have a part in all

153

this, the question crossed his mind for an instant), and he raised his eyes as if trying to understand the whole thing for a moment, once and for all.

Beyond the bend in the river and the green and yellow plain of the fields, beyond the roadway that ran parallel to the river, there was a smooth expanse of hillocks and mounds, of arable land at times and other times of lands peppered by dark splotches of oak trees where the silvery coil of another road wound its way. Sometimes the land was red, a red that was on occasion claret or crimson, and on other occasions it was like freshly spilt blood, a vibrant cinnabar color in stretches, or ferrous hematite, and other times, in the fallow or stubble fields left uncultivated, it was yellow, or rather greenish, low, open scrubland. Beyond the first hillocks, as they gained height, a few ridges were covered with sessile and Pyrenean oaks that had begun to turn yellow and lose their leaves, and along the riverbeds, the leaves of the poplars, raising their lances on high with all the golden splendor of autumn, provided a counterpoint that, in its transitory finiteness, suddenly seemed eternal to him. Far off, in the distance, and it would have been hard to say whether closing it all off or making everything stand out all the more by delimiting it, the great mountains of the cordillera showed off their sharp, blue profiles in the clear, clean light of morning.

He didn't know if he had ever seen such beauty in his entire life, he surprised himself suddenly thinking, or if perhaps *that*, what there is before disappearing, is what true beauty is in the end, what one has had in his sights and has not seen, now that one has it but cannot go on having it, and if, as a result, it might always have been thus, in the face of every moment that is, by its very nature, about to disappear, or if it was only now.

Nor did he know if all of that beauty was in fact there, in space, or at that moment and, therefore, in time, or even if it was truly out there rather than inside him, or perhaps neither without him nor within him but in the attention he paid, which is what enriched things or impoverished them, what broadened and stretched them or narrowed them and made them rigid and numb like his legs just then, or even what helped create them or crush them. The only thing he knew was that he was there right then, at the edge of everything and right before nothing, and in that everything and that nothing that that moment was, still, for him.

But what kind of thoughts are these, he asked himself, what am I doing thinking such things right now? But suddenly it occurred to him, too, that he had gone up there at the exact moment when it had never been more difficult for him to take a single step, when he could move little better than a lame, broken man in his last days, afflicted by some unknown paralysis. I had to wait until the end, when I could barely walk, to come up and see what could be seen from up here, he told himself again. Does that mean something? Do things speak to us, or is it just our need to implore them to say something to us?

He had barely completed these thoughts when he looked down again, over the precipice, still keeping his

vertigo in check, and he saw his road there still, next
to the river, the dirt road of his father, may he rest in
peace, and his grandfather, and his own, too, the road
that seemed to mark a boundary between the fertility
of the earth and the rocky, steep flanks of the mountain,
between the sere and the lush, that white, perfectly
defined path, delicate more than narrow, just a tiny little
thread from up there, one he could navigate even in his
sleep and still tell you precisely where he was or was
not at any given moment, one you could only travel
on foot and, most likely, in silence, but whose breath—
for a moment he was sure that just beyond a bend, the
road continued along past a metalworks and then a tire
retread shop before passing a great, windowless hangar,
a gas station, then an automobile dealership, and an
interchange—seemed to waft curiously all the way up
to where he was, in the least dispersed and the most
inexhaustible, sure way in the world.

Everything up there seemed to reveal to him its
exact opposite, and it was then that he opened his eyes
as wide as they would go so that he could fit into them
all the space around him, so that he could fit the road
and that immensity and even the entire expanse of time
with all its vicissitudes, while simultaneously breathing
in as much air as he could get into his lungs, as they
said his father had done. The vertigo of disappearance
made him wobble slightly for an instant, still at the
cliff's edge, and immediately, with all that vastness in his
eyes, with the breath of the eternal rising off the road
and up toward him, and a strange sense of piety for all
that remained impenetrable, he took one dumbstruck

step, just one, and it was not forward into the abyss but backward, onto terra firma, followed a moment later by another, and then another, all filled with liberating, inaugural astonishment, and as he turned his head to one side, drawn by the shouting that had just begun to reach him, he saw, too, against the background of all those strangely indomitable surroundings and, above all else, all that unbowed opening of his eyes, his son Felipe—he, too, Felipe Díaz—gasping for breath and running for all he was worth to reach him and throw his arms around him.

He said nothing then, either, but suddenly—the pomegranates are opening up down below, and they're as red and ripe as ever, he heard his son say after a short while—he was certain that if he uttered one phrase or began to say anything, regardless of how softly or loudly, words would have regained all the meaning whose restitution they themselves were clamoring for at the top of their lungs.

Trieste, December 2008

157

ABOUT THE AUTHOR

J. Á. GONZÁLEZ SAINZ is a Spanish writer and translator born in Soria in 1956. His latest book is a collection of short stories, *El viento en las hojas* (Anagrama, 2014). Among his other works are the novels *Ojos que no ven* (Anagrama, 2010), *Volver al mundo* (Anagrama, 2003) and *Un mundo exasperado* (Anagrama, 1995), which received the Herralde Novel Prize. In 2005 he was awarded the Castilla y León Literature Prize. He has translated a number of books from Italian to Spanish by authors such as Magris, Del Giudice, Flaiano, Stuparich, Severino, and was founder and director of one of the most important cultural magazines during Spain's Transition from dictatorship to democracy, namely *Archipiélago, cuadernos de la crítica de la cultura (1989-2009)*. He received his degree in Hispanic Philology from the University of Barcelona and has taught Spanish as a Foreign Language for more than thirty years. *None So Blind* is his first work available in English translation.

ABOUT THE TRANSLATORS

HAROLD AUGENBRAUM is an American writer, editor, and translator. He is currently Executive Director of the National Book Foundation, where he established the Innovations in Reading Prizes, the Literarian Award, 5 Under 35, BookUp, National Book Awards on Campus, and the National Book Awards Teen Press Conference. He is a member of the Board of Trustees of *The Common* literary magazine, founded the Proust Society of America, and is former member of the Board of Trustees of the Asian American Writers Workshop and vice chair of the New York Council for the Humanities. Augenbraum has published six books on Latino literature of the United States, translations of Alvar Núñez Cabeza de Vaca's *Chronicle of the Narváez Expedition* and the Filipino novelist José Rizal's *Noli Me Tángere* and *El filibusterismo* for Penguin Classics, and, for the University of Texas Press, the Mexican writer Juan Rulfo's *The Plain in Flames* (with Ilan Stavans). In 2013, Augenbraum edited the *Collected Poems* of Marcel Proust, also published by Penguin Classics.

CECILIA ROSS is an American translator and editor who has spent nearly the entirety of her adult life abroad, residing for the bulk of those years in Madrid, Spain. She has been an editor at Hispabooks since 2014, and her published works include the first ever translation of the poetry of Dorothy Parker into Spanish, *Los poemas perdidos* (Nórdica Libros, 2013, with Guillermo López Gallego). Her translation into English of Beatriz Espejo's *The Egyptian Tomb* is included in a forthcoming anthology for Words Without Borders, and she has also translated a work of nonfiction by the award-winning Mexican investigative journalist Lydia Cacho, *Memoir of a Scandal* (forthcoming). When not working, Cecilia can be found enjoying life, the universe, and everything with her husband and two Spanglish-fluent children.

Lightning Source UK Ltd.
Milton Keynes UK
UKOW02f1837010515

250759UK00002B/2/P